Journeys

A Novel by Rudy Thomas

ISBN-13: 978-0615516028
ISBN-10: 0615516025

Dedicated to Laura Williams, Palm Reader and Spiritualist who convinced me to change this book from its original version,

and to Alyx,
with special thanks to
Cyerra, Enchanta,
& Krystal, readers, writers
& story tellers .

Special thanks to:
Robert (Bobby) Maurice Reneau, Jr., Terry Roger Riley, Steve Wallace, and Phyllis Zachary for their suggestions and their edits.

PRINTED IN THE UNITED STATES OF AMERICA

Old Seventy Creek Press

ISBN-13: 978-0615516028

ISBN-10: 0615516025

Book One

The Slave Girl and the Stallion

Chapter 1

He had reluctantly agreed to attend church with his seventeen-year-old cousin, George Washington Thomas Jefferson, named for two presidents. He had come to Nashville to buy a seven-year-old stallion for his father, a brother to George Washington Thomas Jefferson's mother, Mary. The stallion was from Henry Clay's race winning line of horses, thoroughbreds, genetic lines his father wanted to cross with his own brood mares.

He had not listened to the minister's sermon for he was deep in thought. He had turned eighteen last Wednesday. The trip to Nashville was his father's way of telling him that he was old enough to accept responsibility and was, he imagined, also his father's way of testing him. The stallion would be sold at auction by a Nashville slave trader who bought the horse in Lexington. The stallion was out of Yorkshire and a mare sired by Daniel Boone, the horse his father called the most important horse ever acquired by Clay.

He had not listened to the minister's sermon for he was deep into other thoughts. Across the aisle, a young lady kept smiling at him and he found himself attracted to her—so attracted, in fact, that he planned to speak to her as soon as the preacher finished shouting.

The shouting and his cousin's elbow in his right ribs made him sit straighter. The preacher was red-faced, ranting, and he listened:

"And as I live and teach the truth," the man lost his breath, and then paused. The church endured the silence of his pause while the young lady across the aisle smiled and Cry winked at her. "Our Northern Brethren finance the likes of John Brown. They look down on our way of life. They read the Constitution and this book," the minister shouted, "and say we are wrong. I say the words of this book are the truth..."

"Amen," a voice called out.

"Amen," another voice echoed and more voices chimed.

"This book says we must exhort servants to be obedient unto their masters! This book teaches that servants are to please their masters well...in all things!"

"Amen..."

"Amen..."

Cry, listening intently by now, counted as seventeen other men echoed an amen before the man continued:

"This book teaches that servants should not answer back!"

"Amen..."

"Amen..."

And Cry counted seventeen other men's voices rise up again with the word *amen* repeated throughout the room.

5

"And this book teaches servants should not purloin, but show all good fidelity, and I ask you, my brothers and sisters, what more of truth can any man desire?"

Chapter 2

"Where does Chastity live from here?"

"Too far to walk," his cousin said. "I wasn't the only one who saw you two..."

"Who?" he asked...

"Mother..."

"What did she say, Jeff?" he asked, using a short form of his cousin's last name. That practice also brought his aunt's disapproval.

"She said she was glad you would be leaving tomorrow, Cry," Jeff said, calling his cousin Martin Kreider by his nickname, one his mother also hated.

"Tell me everything she said..."

"She said you both had that look..."

"What look?" Cry asked, knowing his aunt had meant their behavior had been overtly sexual.

"You know..."

"Did she think I was going to down her right there on the church steps and rip her petticoats off?"

"I think she actually thought you were the one in danger," Jeff laughed. "She said Chastity wasn't living up to her name and in church of all places."

"And what did you think?"

"I thought to myself I'm going to marry that girl some day, " Jeff said.

Chapter 3

On the day it happened, she had gone less than a mile from town when she noticed the two men, actually noticed their buggy, newer than any she had ever seen. When she came alongside the horses, one man jumped down.

"Careful, gal," he said of the horses. "They've been known to bite."

She stepped back, not fearing the horse but afraid of the man. She did not have her certificate with her. She had not carried it in over a year. She darted away from the buggy, but the man overtook her and tied her hands together while she was thinking *this cannot be happening to me—* thinking *not on the open street in the light of day,* but it was happening and no one came to help her. The man, smelling worse than old Tom who cleaned out the stables, dragged her to the buggy, paying no heed to her protests. It took both men to get her up and into the vehicle.

The men, slave rustlers from Floyd County, Kentucky, usually stole slaves at night in rural eastern Kentucky and hid them in Campbell's Cave. When their trail had cooled, they exported the black laborers to Clarksville, Tennessee, where they sold them again on Mr. Dunk Moore's slave market. Lewis Robards, a Lexington slave dealer, also used their services. They were on their way home from Lexington where they had sold a young woman they took two nights before in Prestonsburg on Second Avenue not far from a rambling two-story frame house with brick chimneys and a two-story veranda across the front. The house faced the river where they hid their boat. The tall, young woman named Polly had not fought them, for they told her they would take her to Ohio where she would be free and she had trusted them.

Although it was early afternoon when they spied Alyx walking alone, they never hesitated. Their destination had been the tavern, a two-and-a-half story stone building overlooking the Paris public square where they planned to drink Bourbon whiskey and spend some of their money on women or lose it in the billiard room. They sped off with her knowing that in Lexington they would get the most money for her and no one would come after them or to her rescue.

They got her from Paris to Lexington before nightfall and the slave dealer sold her to a Danville slaver who set out immediately; drove a chattel of twelve men, women, and children to Port Isabel on the Cumberland River and put them on a steamboat for Nashville, Tennessee.

Chapter 4

They did not get to Chastity's house the next morning. They went instead to bid on the stallion for Cry's father, Martin. The horse and others, along with mules, would be put on the auction block near the Negro hack drivers' corner at Cedar and Cherry streets. They arrived early. A small crowd milled about, waiting for the sale to begin.

"This hyar Nashville wuz jist uh ruff community, Nashborough, in they wildernezz," an old man shouted, speaking to no one in particular, but everyone within hearing range as he waded through the crowd of buyers on Cherry Street where Will L. Boyd, Jr. sold slaves and horses. "When I cum hyar uh boy with uh few settlerz from the older districtz back East, we all lived in hewed, framed log-housez and twenty er more rough cabinz. That'z all thiz place wuz, boy..."

Cry looked at the man, dressed in a ragged, long coat, one Cry reasoned the man's father or grandfather had worn before the turn of the century, and Cry smiled at the man then looked away.

"Yeah, ya boy," the man said. "I'm talken ta ya."

Cry turned to face the man.

"I'll be eighty-five my next birthday. I wuz born two dayz after they Continental Congress 'dopted they Declarashun of Independance. Parentz named me John

Declaration Jones. Folkz call me Deck. Who might ya be?"

"I'm Cry."

The old man chuckled. "I remember they year Congress set aside money fur they Cumberland Road from Cumberland, Maryland ta Wheeling, Virginia on the Ohio River. That wuz when I lost uh job. You see, Congress outlawed the bringen slavez in ta thiz hyar country. I wuz uh sailor."

Cry raised his eyebrows...

"Not uh slave runner, mind ya. I nary time sailed ta Afrika taken made goods—never picked up human cargo fur they West Indiez. Me, I heped run rum and lasses ta this hyar country."

The old man had captured Cry's interest.

The old man knew he had peaked the young man's curiosity and began to speak with enthusiasm, "I wuz on uh flatboat goen down they Mississippi when that great earth quake at New Madrid, Missouri made the river run backerdz fur several hourz and made Reelfoot Lake on they Tennessee side. Now that wuz uh confusion fur me 'bout equal, it wuz ta they time Mount Tambora erupted, thrown dust up in ta the sky so'z thiz whole world wuz colder fur uh year. Ya ain't from hyar, air you?"

"New York," Cry said.

"Ya uh buyer or uh seller, air you?"

Cry looked at the man, but before he could say anything, the old man continued...

"Thiz slave dealer in Louisville, Kentucky, I worked fur, buyed buckz, wenchez, and picinniez fur the New Orleanz market. That wuz back in 43 when thar must uh been eighty-one dealers in they Louisville Directory. And I worked out uh Lexington most uh last year. That city has about ten thousand people and four firms uh slave dealers, three uh em specialize in thiz hyar kind uh trade, and I reckon thar must uh been eleven individual traders like thiz hyar man what'z holding thiz auction. They air all men of meanz who, like William F. Talbot, can git shed uh cash. Each person they buy seems like they pay too metch money fur em, yet they cart em hyar and most 'specially on south down the Trace. Profits they get on each one uh em when selling ta New Orleans and Texas, other markets fur Kentucky slavez most folks don't know 'bout, makes em a fortune."

"I'm here to buy a horse," Cry stated.

"Which un?"

"The Clay stallion," Cry whispered.

"Don't bid on im, boy," the old man warned.

Cry looked at the old man without saying again that he was going to buy the animal. He had four thousand dollars to spend and a spare thousand in case he needed it, but his father had told him he expected the horse could be bought for less.

"I ain't hyar fur they hoss, boy, iffen that'z what ya thank. See that man over thar with all em folkz round im?"

Cry looked at the tall, strongly built man, but looked away when the man's eyes locked on his.

"Who is he?" Cry asked.

"Who iz he? Well, that man iz Nathan Bedford Forrest," the man spoke softly. "He cum from uh pore rural family and like me ain't got metch book larnin, but he's been uh buyer and uh seller, uh dealer mind ya, fur quite uh spell. He's operated out uh Memphis, Tennessee fur years, whar he'z made uh fortune. Slave tradin's been big business hyar in Nashville since 1850, but Memphis iz they big market place in thiz hyar state. That man'z won uh the richest slave men in they South. Just read this hyar," the man said, reaching a newspaper toward Cry. "I marked hiz ad. See thar what hit sayz..."

FIVE HUNDRED NEGROES WANTED. - We will pay the highest cash price for all good Negroes offered. We invite all those having Negroes for sale, to call on us, at our Mart, opposite Hill's old stand, on Adams Street. We will have a good lot of Virginia Negroes on hand, for sale, in the fall. Negroes bought and sold on commission. HILL & FORREST.

"So," Cry said. "I've read it."

"Now don't get uppity with me, son. Folks say his money from slave trading alone-he also owns big cotton plantations-air more than $50,000," the old man said. "He probably used ta sell more than uh thousand slaves uh year. I heared he quit, but thar he iz. He'z uh leader of hiz community; got lected alderman in 58. He'z cum hyar ta buy everything today, even yore horse, so'z ya best jist cry now and get hit over with."

Cry looked at the old man and frowned. He wanted the man to get out of his face.

"The name'z Deck," the old man reminded him.

The auction never began. Cry expected it to be held on the northeast corner of Cedar and North Cherry where Jeff waited for him. Instead, the man Deck had called Forrest went into the dealer's office before the door opened. In a few minutes, a man came outside.

"There won't be any auction today, folks!" he yelled. "Mr. Forrest has purchased everything. Check back with us in two weeks. We'll have more mules, horses, and slaves by then. Just read the newspaper so you'll know what we get..."

Cry got angry, but he could not vent his anger. He had never been to a slave auction before, but he had attended estate sales in New York. He took Nathan Bedford Forrest to be a shrewd businessman. By going into the office before the auction started, Cry realized *the man saved himself a bundle.*

When the crowd began to clear, Cry looked for his cousin. He saw him across the street talking to the old man. He wondered what the old man was up to. He walked toward them and when he got close, the old man grabbed his left arm.

"Take this hyar with ya and read hit," the old man said and pulled a tattered book from the right pocket of his long coat. "Meet me hyar in they morning 'bout thiz time and we'll see what we can do 'bout that stallion..."

"The horse will be in Memphis by morning," Cry said, " and I'll be in New York."

"No! No, son!" the old man said, moving away. "Ya want they hoss then read—read..."

Chapter 5

When Cry told his aunt after he and Jeff returned from the sale what had happened and asked to spend another day or two, she smiled like his father did. It was the first time he had recognized any resemblance in the two of them. The smile was her only answer.

Before retiring, Cry went upstairs to the room next to Jeff's and lit the lamp by his bed. He looked at the book old Deck had given him, Mary Wollstonecraft's *A Vindication of the Rights of Woman*, published in1792. He had never heard of it, but he read for an hour, soon realizing that the author was protesting the common assumption men have that women exist only to be their playthings.

I'm not like that he thought, but then he remembered how he had flirted with Chastity, thinking *maybe I am.*

As he turned the page, he found a small handbill that he also read:

Fancy gals for sale

Rees W. Porter invites all discriminating buyers to examine the six Kentucky bred Fancy Gals he has for sale. This lot of Fancy Gals will be sold inside the office at 33 Cedar street in Nashville, Tennessee. Come inspect our Fancy Gals and be prepared to buy. This is the one sale you can't afford to miss.

16

Cry realized that the old man who said his name was Deck had not meant for him to read the book but only the ad for some reason. *The man is probably a thief, a huckster,* he thought. Then he thought about the man who outfoxed everyone at the auction and remembered how Deck had talked about him.

Cry blew out the flame in his aunt's oil lamp and got back in bed. He did not fall asleep at once. He kept hearing Deck's parting words to him about reading and his plea for them to meet in the morning. He had not seen the Clay stallion. All he knew about it was its bloodlines.

He's going to try to put a ringer off on me Cry reasoned. He decided that his first thought, the one that the horse would be in Memphis, would prove to be correct.

But why a Fancy Gal auction? he wondered.

Chapter 6

"Where have ya been?" Deck asked as he rushed toward Cry.

There was an urgency to the old man's voice that Cry picked up on at once. He did not answer, thinking instead *maybe I was wrong about him* as they crossed the muddy street.

"Fancy galz ain't sold at auction, er all at once, but singly, er in partiez, az purchaserz may be inclined ta buy," Deck said. "Likewise, fancy galz ain't advertised in classifiedz they way slave traderz in Natchez newspaperz simply announce they availability uh slavez fur purchase. Ya got at least four thousand in gold in that thar belt yore wearin... Mabbe more..."

Cry stopped, a frown on his face.

"Hell'z fire, boy!" Deck raised his voice. "We got ta be on time. Yore kin told me about the gold—mabbe as many as fifty big coinz. I ain't got uh mind ta rob you..."

"*I don't trust you*," Cry thought.

"If ya had had bank notez on ya, ya would uh had no chance at getting that stallion. The only tender they take at uh fancy galz auction iz gold and silver coinz, mostly gold. Now, we air goin in thar and ya have ta do what I say. When we get in thar, thar ain't gonna be no competitive, public spectackle atmosphere lyke an

auction. In thar, buyerz and sellerz air free
ta quietly strike a bargain."

"I didn't come here to buy slaves,"
Cry said.

"Yes, son," Deck said. "Ya did. Jist
like Nathan Bedford Forrest did. Ya did.
Ya got that handbill I gived ya?"

"No," Cry lied.

"Yes ya do, boy! Now hold hit out fur
the doorkeep when ya go in. Ya see, son,
ya got uh nuff gold ta buy mabbe two
fancy galz, but ya only want they good
un..."

"Good one?"

"The best," Deck said. "Ya'll know
hur az soon az ya see hur. Now, I'll go
straight ways ta the seller when he cumz
up and stand by 'im. You come up ta uz
and tell him ya'll give 'im $4,000 in gold
fur yore fancy gal. Forrest iz here fur all
them galz ya'd better believe, but ya get
that gal and ya'll have that Clay stallion."

Cry took the handbill from the
inside pocket of his jacket and Deck
smiled, walking quickly away. Cry waited
a few minutes, thinking *this is crazy. I'd
be a fool to go in there.* He turned and
stepped into the street with the voice in
his head asking: *What is a fancy gal?* He
turned back toward the building, one of a
cluster of rough wooden buildings, near
the Negro hack drivers' corner at Cedar
and Cherry streets. He heard voices
behind him and turned to see the man
Forrest and four other men approaching.

19

Maybe... Just maybe he thought, but he did not have time to think for he meant to act first today.

"You got an invite, boy?" the doorkeeper, a tall man dressed in a tailored suit, asked.

"Here," Cry said, extending his right hand.

The man took the handbill and pointed across the room toward a closed door.

Cry walked along the hallway, thinking *the man has a tailored, New York suit, one father buys, one similar to three he bought last month when we were in the city. I can't remember the tailor's name, but I recognize his unique and unmistakable craftsmanship...*

"Mr. Forrest," Cry heard the doorkeeper greet the group of men, "I believe your buyer is the last. We will begin at once..."

"Last shall be furst," a man's voice Cry took to be Nathan Bedford Forrest's answered.

Entering through the wide door into an open room large enough to be a courtyard, Cry scanned the crowd, counting fifteen men, partially enclosing a line of six woman dressed in black gowns, each holding a white parasol with her left hand, gloved in white like New York society women wear.

The doorkeeper is Mr. Porter he thought. He had not told Deck that he was late because he had gone to 72 Broad Street where G. H. Hitchings had held an earlier sale. He had remained there only long enough to observe the sale of a few field hands, each dressed in what one buyer from Mississippi had said to his woman friend was the usual uniform of slaves in the market. Cry noted how each slave held a fashionably shaped, black fur hat; wore a roundabout and trousers of coarse corduroy velvet that he had seen Irish laborers wear, arriving at Ellis Island, complete with good vests, strong shoes, and white cotton shirts. Each stood perfectly still, and silent in close order, while some gentlemen were passing from one to another examining them.

The women in front of him were chatty and Cry could see what a fancy gal was. They were not light-skinned, mulattos. They were as white as Chastity and elegant in appearance, their black hair shiny, their eyes dark except for the fourth one in line. Her eyes were of the lightest blue.

The doorkeeper nodded at Cry but did not speak as he passed. Cry saw Deck move toward the man and began to amble in their direction.

"When were you in New York City, Mr. Porter?" Cry asked.

Deck's mouth dropped open.

"Last month, young man?" Mr. Porter answered. "And you."

"September as well," Cry said. "You and my father have the same tailor."

"You saw me there?"

"No, sir. I recognize the style, the tailor is first rate..."

"And who are you?"

"Sorry, sir," Cry said, extending his hand. "I am Martin Kreider."

Mr. Porter studied him, then gave a quick jerk of his head, asking: "And what do you do for a living, Martin?"

"I help my father and go to school, sir..."

"And your father?"

"Since 1837, he has manufactured John Deere plows," Cry said.

"I know..." Mr. Porter started to speak; stopped, then continued: "A technological leap forward that steel moldboard. It has brought into production prairie soil farmers could not till. Extend my regards to your father for his taste in apparel and his outstanding product."

"I shall, Mr. Porter..."

"What may I do for you, Martin?"

"I want to buy the blue-eyed woman," Cry said.

"You do now, do you? How much do you expect to buy her for?"

"Three thousand in gold coins, sir..."

Mr. Porter looked at Deck. Deck cocked his head and shrugged his shoulders.

"Do you believe this young man, Deck?"

"Can't say az I do, Mr. Porter?"

"I have half a mind to ask him, Deck, if his father knows he's here. What do you think he'll say if I ask him thirty-five hundred in gold, Deck?

"What would ya say, boy?" Deck asked.

"I'd say let's go into the office and see if I've got that much gold on me," Cry said.

"Follow me, Martin. Deck, you circulate and tell Mr. Forrest to join me in my office as soon as young Kreider leaves. You know, son, I have a reputation for being careful of the interests of the slaves I sell. I allow field hands the opportunity to choose a master and often help them decide which one is best. I treat my fancy gals the same way. I reserve the right to talk to her about you. Being the young man you are, I can understand why you want my best Fancy Gal, and you've just bought her... You stand here so she can see you and I'll speak with her before we see your gold..."

Chapter 7

"And whom should I say is calling?" Cry, descending the stairs, heard his aunt ask when she opened the door.

"Mr. Porter and Mr. Nathan Bedford Forrest," Cry recognized the man's voice with whom he had done business earlier in the day. His heart began to pound.

"If you'll wait in the parlor there to your right," his aunt said, "I'll send him in at once."

Cry took the final three steps quickly. He did not want Mr. Porter to tell his aunt about the Fancy Gal he had purchased.

"Hello, Martin Kreider," Mr. Porter said, extending his right hand.

"Good evening, Mr. Porter," Cry shook the man's hand.

"May I introduce Mr. Nathan Bedford Forrest?"

"Mr. Forrest," Cry nodded his head and extended his right hand.

"Air ya up fur uh night in gaslight?" Mr. Forrest asked.

Cry cocked his head toward the left for the question was not one he had expected. Suddenly the only thing he could think about was the river front.

"Are you headed for the jungle?" Cry asked.

Mr. Forrest began to speak again with his dialect becoming less distracting,

"Nashville by gaslight, and Nashville by day light, air as widely different as secesh and Union..."

Mr. Porter chimed in, "In daylight, our goodly city looks very much like a whipped dog. Nobody has a kind word or look for it, and it sulks around street corners like a defeated politician."

Cry knew about the Nashville river front, that section of the city had developed an undesirable quarter called *The Jungle*. It was a district of cheap saloons, brothels, and hideouts for criminals. It was not the lower levels of society alone that patronized the institutions of ill repute. Aristocrats held keys to prostitutes' doors and played cards with professional gamblers. Wild oats had been sowed there by many of the young men he and Jeff knew.

"Is this about the Fancy Gal, Mr. Forrest?" Cry asked.

"I reckon hit iz, son, and ya can call me Bedford..."

"We should retire to the front porch, sir," Cry said.

The two men nodded their heads as though realizing Cry's tenuous position and followed him from the room.

"Sure you don't want to go with us tonight, Cry? This City of Rocks at night has a pleasant way, which is as productive as anything you have ever seen. With evening comes activity and crowded streets-music and jollity; and sometimes as we contemplate the surging masses, from one point to another, we forget that we are in ancient Nashville, and unconsciously inquire, with our optics, for Fifth avenue, City hall park, Broadway, places you know well," Mr. Porter stopped speaking to breathe.

That charm," Cry said, "might be lasting, if it were not that there are no women I wish to be seen with in the midst of the human ocean of which you speak, especially along river front."

"The jungle ain't as bad as some folks make it out to be," Mr. Porter said. "The women there don't go to the theater. Men like us can get you in and out of there without any trouble. We can even leave you there for the night and you can come out when it's day."

The man's words went against everything Cry knew about the water front. He had been in the jungle with Jeff and two or three others over the past three or four summers and knew it was always a dangerous section for the unsuspecting, the uninitiated. It housed the painted ladies of the street and provided quarters for card sharks, pickpockets, petty thieves, and confidence men. It was almost impossible for a man to walk through the jungle without being confronted—even accosted by women.

Scarcely a night went by that the jungle did not cause a disturbance in the streets. Hard liquor, over-indulgence in particular, caused the majority of the problems, as did the inherent vulgarity of the place. Always the women there on the streets caused much of the chaos.

"I want ya to know that I only drink whiskey fur medicinal purposes and I love my Mary so the women thar don't interest me. I do like uh good game of chance. What say you we play uh hand to decide this?"

"No, sir," Cry said.

"Air ya Abolitionist?" Forrest asked.

"No, sir..."

"Air ya familiar with George Nicholas and John Breckinridge?"

"No, sir," Cry repeated.

"Do ya think of slavery as uh positive good?"

"I don't know, sir," Cry said.

"Uh necessary evil?" Forrest asked.

"Again, sir," Cry said, "I do not know."

"Do ya know the biblical defense of slavery iz tied to God's chosen people, the Jews, owen slaves, so slavery ain't no mortal sin, been, in fact, ordained by God?"

"That was the preacher's sermon Sunday," Cry said.

The men laughed and Cry smiled.

"Old Deck told me you bought the Fancy Gal for a reason," Mr. Porter said, "but he wouldn't say what that reason was. Now Bedford here had a reason for wanting her, too..."

"I'll be up front with ya, son. I had me enuff uh this business early this year. Man makes enuff money ta do him and he needs ta quit. I cum here fur two sales— one yisterdee and this un. When I solt my real-estate, livestock, and slave business, I went back home ta Mississippi. I have recently moved back ta Memphis and I'm an Alderman. I don't mean ta take up the slave trade business no more. Man in my party wants yore Fancy Gal. After he talked ta hur, she wants ta go with 'im. I aim ta buy her from ya... I wanted you ta go with us ta meet im and the other buyers who cum hyar with me from Memphis."

"She's not for sale," Cry said.

"Hell!" Mr. Porter exclaimed.

"Everything has uh price, son..."

"She's not for sale," Cry repeated.

"What if I tell ya I have ten thousand in gold coins hyar on me?"

"I'd tell you ten thousand in gold coins cannot buy her," Cry said.

"Let's say I got twenty thousand in gold and bank notes?

"Same answer," Cry said.

Nathan Bedford Forrest smiled.

Cry cocked his head to the left then looked straight at the man.

"I seen you at the auction, didn't I?"

"Of course you did," Mr. Porter said.

"Not yorn," Forrest said. "Yisterdee's auction... I take hit yore uh stock trader like me. Perhaps we can dicker."

28

"Perhaps," Cry said.

"I'll trade you the horse and my pick of uh slave gal fur yore property," Forrest said.

Cry swallowed quickly.

"Deal?" Forrest asked.

Cry hesitated for a moment then extended his right hand.

The men walked down the steps and Cry turned toward the well-lit house. Something struck his right shoulder- something like a stone but he did not see anyone. He looked toward the center of Nashville and stood thinking before he went inside.

He remembered the first time that he went to visit the recently completed new capitol. He went and looked at it and found, perhaps for the first time in his life outside New York, that there are such things as lines of beauty, that strength can be found in pillar and arch, that poetry can be written with stone.

Viewing the new capitol building helped erase his memories of the plain sections of the city the men had set off for, the river front with its park-like landscape, the gas works with its thong of men, and the jungle. He appreciated his aunt' s house near the business district where his uncle walked daily to his upscale hardware store with its warehouse for farm implements, tools, and grains.

Although he had not seen Edwin Booth as Hamlet at the Gaiety, he resolved to catch the actor's performance on Broadway. Women who came to his aunt's house talked of Booth as though there was no other actor whenever the stage was mentioned. His hope was that the actor who was synonymous with the name Hamlet would be in New York in the spring.

"Is that you, Deck?" Cry asked when he heard a noise in the bushes.

"Ya got that right," the old man said.

Chapter 8

"Thanks for putting up with me," Cry told his aunt as he hugged her.

"It was good to have you with us. Don't be a stranger, Cry. Your uncle Wash said they might see you at the depot," his aunt said. "They've got a flat car of freight to unload and deliver. Wash says he wishes you could drive, but he understands you have the stallion and want to get it home."

"I need to, Aunt Mary," Cry said.

"Wash says you can handle a team like a mule skinner," she laughed. "I've packed you ham and biscuits. Give my love to everyone."

"I will," Cry promised, picking up his bag, thinking: *I can't take the train now* as he left the house and walked toward Deck's place

The old man was sitting on the porch when Cry arrived. He did not get up nor speak at once as Cry climbed the six wooden steps, dropped his bag on the oak planks and sat in the ladder back chair beside him.

"Ya look like yore ready ta travel," Deck observed, "but appears like ya ain't metch thrilled 'bout hit."

"What am I going to do with the girl?" Cry asked.

"Yore gonna take hur with ya on that train ta Louisville like we planned... The furst thru train come down from Louisville jist this year."

"Can't take the train," Cry said.

Deck squinted then said, "Like I tole ya last night on yur uncle's porch after yore company left..."

"Did you come with Mr. Porter and Mr. Forrest and hide in the bushes while they came in to talk me into going out with them?"

"I came in from they river side of they house and seen they three of ya on they porch. I just hid in they dark, listnen ta yore trade. When they left, I hit ya with that thar marble."

"Is that what it was?" Cry asked.

"Jist like this little feller," Deck answered, taking another marble from his pocket. "I allays carry uh marble fur luck."

"My aunt Mary carries a buckeye..."

"Heap uh folks, country born ones at least, do hit. I was 'bout ta say we decided ya and they gal and they stallion would ride they train ta Louisville. As I was 'bout ta say, ya can't leave her in Nashville like ya want uh. Free slaves have ta leave they state. That's they law..."

"I'm giving her to you," Cry said.

Deck got a wild look on his face, one that surprised Cry for it was a look of fear.

"Naw," Deck said, flatly.

"My uncle, my cousin and a crew of men are at the depot this morning. I can

take the horse, but not the girl. You keep
her, sell her and put the money in your
pocket. After all, I wouldn't have the Clay
stallion if you hadn't helped…"

"If ya want ta pay me," Deck said,"
ya can give me uh couple uh gold coins,
but not the gal."

"It's her or nothing," Cry bargained.

"Ya go down ta Porter's place and git
yore property, all of hit, and go down ta
they river. Catch ya they furst steamboat
headed up river! Git!"

Cry could not believe what he had
heard the old man say.

"Git! I say…"

Cry got up, retrieved his bag and
started down the steps. When he stepped
into the muddy street, he turned to look at
Deck. The old man shook his head and
waved him on. Cry took two gold coins
from his pocket and tossed them up
toward Deck. They landed, but Deck did
not immediately pick them up.

Chapter 9

Going up the Cumberland in the sternwheeler was not what Cry wanted to be doing. When the captain told him as he boarded with the horse and the slave girl that it would probably take two days to get to Celina, and two or three days more to get to Port Isabel, he must have looked as downhearted as he felt.

What was it that the captain said? he asked himself—then he remembered...

"Two fine pieces of property you have there...

That's what the man had said. Property... and something about how lucky they were that it had rained or else they wouldn't be navigating upstream in winter...

Two deck hands led the stallion left toward the paddle wheels beyond which two empty barges were secured to be towed upriver where they would be reloaded with coal.

The captain had said: *There's no room at the inn. The aft cabin is full of ladies. The forward cabin near the bar is full of men.*

Without hesitating, Cry gave the man a gold coin. The captain bit on it and motioned for a crew member and talked softly to the man. Cry and the slave girl followed the deck hand, who spoke a mixture of German and broken English, past the boiler deck above the main deck to the narrower hurricane deck. Its cabin contained a stateroom, officer quarters, and the steamer office. The man escorted them to the steamer office and left with only a nod of his head. The office was small, but it also had a bed Cry assumed to be the captain's.

Cry placed his bag on the floor and walked down to the main deck, the cargo area where the stallion was the only livestock boarded. The animal jerked his head up quickly when the three short blasts from the steamboat's whistle signaled the boat's departure. As the sternwheeler strained against the downstream currents, he watched the muddy river flow. It would be later in the day that he would hear the *begging whistle*: one long, two short, one long, two short blasts that would announce the boat's approach to a ferry or landing where more goods and passengers would be boarded as other goods and people departed.

From a merchant at the dock, he had bought enough shelled corn and oats to feed the stallion on the trip up river, but he had not brought food for himself or the girl. He knew he could buy food on the boat, but he did not know how he would be able to sleep in the same room with the young woman.

Cry walked the deck and looked into the Cumberland river for most of that day. He wished he had faced his uncle, his cousin, and the men at the depot. The train to Louisville would have been faster and more comfortable for the three of them.

There were many passengers on the deck even though it was cold. The front that brought rain and put a chill in the air also raised the river a few feet below flood stage. He realized that they, mostly men, would be on the deck until they reached their destinations. As darkness approached, he wondered whether the captain would take port for the night at one of the many ferry crossings or landings along the Cumberland.

How slow the sternwheeler is he thought. *How like a snake's trail the river is.*

He did not even know the woman's name. He had left her in the room alone, knowing that she might decide to leave the ship if he gave her the opportunity. But he had seen that the raging river afforded few places where she could safely jump— sandbars, gravel bars, or fallen trees. The look that Deck had given him when he offered to give her to him had made him wonder about her. He found himself hoping that he would go back upstairs and find that she had disappeared in the dense timber lining the river bank.

Cry made his way to the passenger quarters on the boiler deck. It was painted white, trimmed in gilt and adorned with turned wood columns. Overhead were glass skylight panes. Besides serving as bar and passenger quarters, the deck contained a lounging area and dining hall. He went to the end of the dining room and asked a woman with a white apron for two plates. The cook, a large Negro woman with her head wrapped in white cloth that matched her apron and her cotton dress, went into the small galley. In a short time, she came out, carrying two plates heaped with potatoes, brown beans, roast beef and cornbread.

"Ain't no charge," she said softly. "Jest leaf yor plates outside yor dor and Ise cum by for um...Ise tole yor gal to do duh same wid duh udder thangs she axed for..."

"Did she come down here?"

"Naw, baas, Ise bay duh won what wen oop dere. Git an wid ya, now den, massa..."

Massa Cry thought. *I am a master, an unwilling one...*

Chapter 10

After they had eaten, Cry put the plates beside the washbasin outside the small room. When he closed the door, he turned to face the woman who had a look of defiance that quickly faded as fear took its place.

Before he spoke, he went to the lamp and extinguished the flame that had blackened the globe. He took off his boots and his trousers then made his way through the dark to the bed. As his eyes adjusted to the darkness, he could see her profile as she undressed.

"If it's okay with you," he said, "I'll take the inside."

There was no answer. After a few minutes, Cry felt the feather tick give way under her weight. She sat on the edge of the bed, naked, with what he took to be a letter opener in her right hand. In the half-light that filtered into the room from the fires hung over the side of the boat, Cry watched her lift her legs; studied the shadowed lines of her left thigh; and felt excitement build tension in his chest—a strange tension similar to what he felt at Niagara Falls when he watched a man walked a tightrope with zest and verve.

The man walked the swaying rope without a safety net strung beneath him. He remembered how that added element of danger had added to the intensity of his feelings.

It's worse than ever here he thought...

"People call me Cry," he said. "What do they call you?"

"Nigger," she answered.

He was astonished by the sound of her voice.

"What is your name?"

"Alyx," she said.

"Alex is a man's name," he said...

"A-l-y-x," she spelled her name. "My mother gave it to me when I was born. She loved a man named Alex before my father. That's why she gave me the name."

"And your family name?"

"Day," she spoke English with a distinct American intonation, the kind an educated woman would speak. Her voice was soft. "Pap used ter laugh—say we would never be in dey dark. He was so wrong. Ise ban n darknuss sence Ise ban solt..."

"Lie down, Alyx Day," he said.

"Yassa, massa," her voice deepened as she did, for she spoke the slave dialect.

"I don't aim to dishonor you," he said. "Lie down and tell me a story..."

"Uh story?" she asked... "What kind uh story do uh nigger tell her master?"

"I am not your master. You are a free woman, Alyx Day. As soon as we get to a clerk's office in Kentucky, I'll do the paperwork. I couldn't leave you in Tennessee."

Alyx did not speak. Cry could hear the river lapping against the hull of the boat. The silence was broken by her sobbing...

"Lie down and tell me your story, Alyx," Cry repeated.

"Why?" Alyx asked.

"Because I want to know who you are," he said.

"Why would you set me free?"

"What would you have me do with you?"

"I expect you will rape me," she said, "then sell me or take me to your plantation."

"Plantation," he laughed. "I live in New York. We don't have plantations there nor slaves."

"Are you taking me to New York?"

"I'll take you wherever it is you want to go," he said. "Where would you like for me to take you?"

She stood, pulled the cover down, and slid beneath it before she said, "I have a paper in Paris that says I'm a free woman..."

"Paris, France?" he asked.

"Kentucky!" she said.

"Never heard of it," he said. "Where is it?"

"Near Lexington," she said.

"Then I will take you to Paris," he said.

"No!"

"Where do you want to go?"

"Berea," she said. "They have a school there. Whites and blacks, women and men get to study together..."

"Is Berea your home?"

"I have no home," she sobbed.

"Home is not necessarily where you belong," Cry said, "but where you were born, the faces you first saw around you, and the place where you only cry when you are hurt, physically or emotionally. Tell me a story, Alyx. Tell me your story."

"My father owned a farm in Kentucky," she began. "It joined my grandfather's farm and our house fronted the Green River. My mother was a slave; bought at auction. Her father was white. Her mother had a white father. All my grandmothers going back to 1733 or 1734 when there were slave uprisings in Jamaica—four, maybe five generations back had white fathers."

"That would have to make you white, then..."

"It makes me a slave," she said. "Five, six, or seven generations back or maybe even before that, my mother said I had a grandmother's family and they were found living east of the Shannon river when Cromwell invaded Ireland. His quest was for the Irish Revolutionaries and their families who dared oppose the British. The English had seized Jamaica to set up British plantations. The punishment for my family's crime, living where they pleased, was either death or slavery for women in the West Indies and death, banishment, or imprisonment in New Zealand or Australia for the men. I don't know the woman's name, but she was Irish. The masters on their island, English plantations made white Irish female servants like her sleep with a black to get pregnant or marry one so she and her children would become black Irish slaves. My mother told me that story the night before we got sold. I never knew my mother was a slave until Pa died or that her family was a lot of slaves or that I would became one myself. She had six girls and a boy who died when he was born. I was the fourth child born to her and my father. She always called him George, his first name, and we call him Pa and her Ma. We called our grandfather Pap and our grandmother Memaw. Memaw was from England. She taught all of us. I can read, write, and I love Science. I'd like to go to England someday. At least when I was with my grandmother, I always said I would sail across the Atlantic Ocean like she did. I never knew my family tree was cursed until my father drowned rafting a load of hogs when I was fourteen. Memaw died that year, too, and Pap got bitter. She was only sixty-nine when she took sick. Without a doctor, she was gone in less than two months. Pap sold our farm and his farm and since he was moving to Indiana to live with Pa's sister, he sold the seven of us because Indiana is a Free State. I have not seen or heard from any of them..."

"I'm sorry," Cry said, but he knew the words did little to comfort her.

He did not fall asleep at once. She lay on her right side as he did. With only a few inches separating them, he heard her sigh. He heard her breathe. He knew she could not sleep either. Her story was one that he would never have imagined. He could not envision that any obstacles or difficulties could ever come into his own life that would ever equal hers.

He felt like she had brought the letter opener to bed to protect herself from him. The thought made him uneasy. He rolled over on his left side, putting as much distance between them as he could.

Chapter 11

Cry woke when the pilot blew the sternwheeler's whistle and began to move the boat at dawn. He rolled on his right side and looked at the woman. Neither the straining blasts of the whistle nor the steam engine shaking the boat as the big wheel began to rotate forward awakened her.

Cry looked at her face, calm for the moment and fair skinned it was, white tinged with pink. The only hint to her African lineage was on her lip, the upper sporting a slight puff to it. Her dark black hair was no more curly than that of his five, red-haired aunts and their many children, his cousins males and females. He did not have red hair, but there was a natural curl to his ash brown locks.

He realized for the first time in his life that America was not one country. It was one country in name but two in regard to slavery.

That's just my father talking in my head he thought.

His father had spoken about slavery *being the gap*—and the words he heard were his father's spoken at the table over coffee: *between the committed and the indifferent.*

He realized he was an indifferent one from the North where slavery might as well be an old wives' tale.

Alyx, sleeping, appealed to him. He was tempted to touch her but guilt overtook him as he remembered the things he had read in the book Deck gave him before the auction. He thought about Chastity and the way their eyes connected at church. Where Alyx was concerned, he would be as good as his word, for his father had always taught him to value honesty.

He could not deny, however, that Alyx, sleeping, her left shoulder exposed almost to her breast, aroused him.

You promised her...

The boat, having reached its top speed, no longer creaked.

She was given to me as boot between the horse and the Fancy Gal he told himself and he felt ashamed— ashamed that he was aroused but not so very ashamed because she was beautiful— *as beautiful as any woman on Broadway...*

Slavery is not on my map of human relations he told himself—amazed with his original thought.

Slavery is an unmapped area in my head he thought. *It is uncharted in my heart...*

Alyx pulled the cover over her shoulder. She did not speak. She did not open her eyes. He watched her, realizing that there had not been a meeting of eyes between them, realizing that they were strangers exchanging silences...

"Tell me a story," he said.

To his surprise, she told him about her abduction in Paris and how the men got her from Paris to Lexington before nightfall and how the slave dealer sold her to a Danville slaver who drove a chattel of twelve men, women, and children to Port Isabel on the Cumberland River and put them on a steamboat for Nashville, Tennessee.

"This very boat," she whispered and a chill ran through him.

He understood why the woman had not charged him for their food...

"I know how to get from Fort Isabel," she said, "to Berea."

Alyx got out of bed, making no attempt to cover her nakedness, holding a dagger, not a letter opener as he had thought when she came to bed. She did not look toward Cry. Watching her, he saw the scars on her back, wide ugly ones...

While she dressed, he thought about Nashville to keep from thinking about her—*impure thoughts* he could hear his aunt's voice as plain as though she were in the cabin—yet, he kept thinking about having spent the night with her, a night he would not be able to relate to his family.

He had planned at the church to ask Chastity to go to the park with him even though it was winter. Bell Meade Park contained some deer, a buffalo, an elk, and a water-ox. It was so cold the day he wanted to take her that they would not have been able to take a picnic supper of ham, sandwiches of various kinds and shapes, pickles, cold chicken, and a bottle of claret or Scotch ale.

Picnics are for summer and Chastity is for Jeff he reminded himself.

In the winter the streets of Nashville get deep in mud and there are days when the city appears almost deserted except for a few children who brave the weather in order to play hop scotch and roll hoops.

He had heard more than one traveler say that the city's virtue could only be seen in the rare beauty of its women.

He looked at Alyx. Even in the dress they had given her at the slave market before the sale that never happened because Nathan Bedford Forrest bought every slave, horse and mule, she was beautiful. Guilt flooded through him again like a river out of its banks. He could not imagine how she must feel knowing she was neither black nor white—knowing she had no possessions of her own except the dagger...

He looked at her and knew that what he had felt at church with Chastity did not compare to his temptation at the moment.

Chapter 12

As he left the room headed toward the stern where the privy was located, overhanging the two-part paddlewheel which would flush his waste away, Cry noticed that the plates had been removed.

The blue and white pitcher and washbasin, too he thought... *Alyx coming to bed like a bride... The dagger...*

He could not remember ever having been so confused about ideas. The idea of being sexual was not new to him, but his idea of it was so different from what Alyx had experienced. He understood her story only by what had happened to her...He could not believe how much the idea of being sexual; yet, refusing to be male had helped him see things, feel things—come face to face with himself during the night...He was unable to imagine how any man could justify rape. *She expected me to rape her* he thought. He shook his head left to right; touched his left ear to his shoulder and then his right ear against his other shoulder. He left the privy and went to feed the stallion.

As he watched the stallion eat the corn and oat mixture, he admired the animal's eyes. They were alive. He looked at the horse and realized that he had not yet looked at the papers, the bloodlines with its registered name.

"From this morning on," he told the stallion, "I will call you Forrest."

He smiled at his lack of originality then glanced to see if Forrest had water. When he saw that the wooden, white oak, half-barrel was almost empty, he found a large cedar bucket and took it to the side of the boat and filled it from the river, flowing clearer now than it had the day before.

He went to the dining area. Although he could smell tobacco smoke, the room was empty. The cook came out of the galley and smiled.

"Massa, Cry," she said. "Ise dun tuk brekfurst ta yore room."

Alyx has told her my name he said to himself.

"Tell me about Alyx," he said.

"Doan know nuttin," she said.

"Tell me about Alyx," he repeated.

"Dat gal got uh yadicone haintin hur..."

"What's a yadicone?"

"Womun burths uh chile... Duh chile die... Womun burths anudder chile, she gots to gib hit duh exaxt name or duh furst chile bay avil haint un cum lib insides duh mudder or wurse duh new chile. Now git ouda hyer... Go et for duh victels gat kolt..."

Chapter 13

"Tell me a story," Cry said when he had finished eating.

"Which story?" Alyx asked.

The knife and the scars Cry thought, but kept silent, looking into her eyes for the first time.

She looked back at him, unblinking through eyes neither black like the stallion's pupils nor brown like his father's. He had imagined that they would be dark. Her eyes were green, with yellow and brown spots.

She looked away for a moment and began to speak, "When Memaw first crossed the ocean she was a Columbus. She only crossed it once though. She was the daughter of a Duke or so she told us..."

"Did you believe her?"

"Memaw was the daughter of a Duke," she said with authority. "She came to Virginia when her brother inherited their father's estate... Said if she had crossed it twenty-five times, none of the other trips could have equaled that first experience. It was a sensation that never wore off. She still felt as fresh a sense of having been a part of something extraordinary, on making land, upon her first voyage even the morning she died. She made me want to discover for myself that there is really another side to the ocean; that is the astonishing thing. It will never happen, in my case. I am on a steamboat going up river with no hope of stepping foot on her continent which this stupidest of boats could not miss, if it could only sail far enough..."

"I would think," Cry interrupted, "that geographies convince only the brain, not the senses, that the globe is round; and since I have no personal experience to draw upon, I believe it to be as wonderful as she suggested it to be."

Alyx looked at him, squinted, then smiled a cautious smile.

"You wear that well," he said.

"It's a slave's dress," she said, "the one they gave me for the sale..."

"I meant your smile," he said.

She frowned...

He wrinkled his forehead...

"A slave wants to get rid of the slave market look at once," she said.

"I will ask the cook where I can buy you some new clothes," he said.

"Where the Obey and the Cumberland rivers meet," she said.

"Then I will buy you a new dress when we get there. You are not a slave, Alyx. I am a student. When I get to New York, I'll be going back to school. When we get you to Berea, you will be a student, a free woman going to school..."

"I can't believe you'll do that. I don't have my paper with me like your horse does. What's to keep you from selling me.

Nothing... I am property and a person, but I can never again be as I was..."

"How long have you dwelt within this unbroken loneliness not of sea and sky, this peculiar institution as it is called in polite circles?"

"Pap sold me six years ago and nothing since that day has been solid in the universe like the bit of painted wood on which we float. All I have left of being a human being is my Memaw's dagger. I can't believe that suddenly one morning something will loom high and cloudlike far away, and you will say to me that it is the land, Berea. You must take me to be ignorant..."

"Hardly," he said. "I take you to be worthy of no less."

"It is not the story I meant to tell you," she said.

"Nor the one I wanted to hear," he told her.

Chapter 14

Cry had not known that Port Isabel was the head of low-water steam navigation on the Upper Cumberland, 358 miles above Nashville Wharf. He heard it from two men when he picked up food at eleven o'clock. While he waited for the cook to fix two plates for supper as she called it, the captain came down to the dining room. He had moored at Carthage for the night. He was in good spirits.

"Folks call me Captain Milliken," he said, extending his hand.

"Martin Kreider," Cry said, exerting pressure equal to that which the captain had squeezed on his right hand.

"The river is great," he said, looking at Cry. "I live at Paducah but I own steamers and packet lines on the Mississippi, Tennessee, Ohio and Cumberland Rivers. I like this river better than the big one. *Noble Ellis* passed us as we docked. Captain Muse don't usually make long runs. River being up like this brought him down no doubt... He's headed home. Lives on a big hill up close to Port Isabel. I don't pilot at night these days— just hang out torch baskets when we land. I'm moving to Texas for good. Got me a sickness... At low tide, sixteen shoals and bars rise out of the water between where we started and where we want to be. We're in a wide valley here running downstream into the Central Basin. Upstream, the river is no more than 600 feet wide and the valley narrows to half a mile or less."

"How many sternwheelers on the river?" Cry asked.

"We're in high times all around, son," he answered. "Things have to go down to Nashville. Barges and boats like this that run shallow bring tobacco, whiskey, cotton, hogs, corn, chickens, eggs, hides, furs, molasses, and meats. I'd say two, three, four hundred boats in all take those things and lumber, walnuts, sang, other herbs, staves, ax handles, cross-ties... You name it. I've been next to many of them floating palaces of sin if you know what I mean?"

"I know," Cry agreed. "I thought we would make better time than we are..."

"Steamboat in 1853 made the trip from New Orleans to Louisville in fourteen hours. Used to take forty or more. Do you know a river has tides like the ocean?"

"No," Cry answered.

"Well, son," the captain said," it does. This tide is what we call the Christmas tide. There's a spring tide, a summer tide, and a fall tide. Rain upstream rules the tide. Heavy rains up beyond Port Isabel start down river, dropping maybe two inches or more in its flow of one hundred to one hundred twenty miles. I've heard it said that

Smith's Shoals drops fifty-five feet in eight miles. It's the worst piece of water on this river. Boats can't go upriver past Port Isabel for the drop is eleven inches and more coming on down to it. Heavy rains create the flood tide, but this here Christmas tide comes along with the November and December rains. Folks upstream wait for it, plan for it all autumn. It's how they get their candy and do-dads for the family. That's why we're stopping at every port, ferry, and river crossing like we are. When the folks hear that whistle blow, they come out of the woods, the hollows. We load about as much on going up as we off load. We could make good time on any other tide. Do you know what I'm smelling?"

"No," Cry said.

"Horse manure," the captain said. "Ain't nothing like it. Would you mind if I take your stallion out for a ride before it gets too dark?"

"Not at all," Cry said. "I've been meaning to ask if it would be possible to take him out. I'll eat then clean up his stall. I didn't know whether you would take him with us, but I'm glad you did."

"I'll tell you, son, I'll haul anything. Only thing I ain't hauled has been the circus. You eat then clean up the horse shit," the captain laughed. "I'll bring him back or you can have the boat..."

"I sure don't need the boat," Cry said.

"I guess a hundred twenty dollar boat ain't much of a trade for a horse like that, is it?"

"I didn't mean that," Cry said.

"It's the truth though. All it cost me to build this thing was the labor. Cut my own timber; sawed my own pattern; and put it together. Your woman don't come down much," the captain said, " and you don't mingle with the other passengers. I can't say as you two ain't better off up there. You don't hear the engine hiss and roar as much that way. Engine has to be on the main deck so the cowl rides high. For a steamboat to navigate this Cumberland it can't ride low like the fancy boats on the Mississippi. It takes a flat bottom packet like this to move upstream fast. The workaday Tennessee steamboats going down river are small, three-hundred-ton, low-draft but drawing up to ten feet draft keeps them from coming up here. The average life span of a boat on these waters is five years. I've got a crew of twelve, including me, a pilot, engineer, mate, a mud clerk, and deck hands. Sometimes my hands are Irish and German immigrants. Free blacks and slaves have worked aboard this steamer."

"My sister stays sick," Cry said, not knowing whether the word *woman* meant wife or slave...

The captain smiled and Cry knew the man meant slave.

"There's a place up river called Free Hills. My cook's from there. She's meaner than a snake. You best watch your sister. She might disappear in that wilderness," the captain laughed and got up to leave.

Cry looked toward the kitchen. The cook came to the doorway with two plates of food.

"Now pay no heed ter dey cap'n. He dun made hisself uh liar. Ise as tame as uh kitt'n," she smiled.

Chapter 15

It was not what Cry expected. Alyx was on top of him when she kissed him. He could smell her body, feel her hair on his cheeks, hear her breath, her fevered, hurried breathing near his right ear, and hear his heart, beating, pounding...

At first, he was embarrassed, not at what she was doing—not with her, but for her. He had only kissed one girl and she was timid—nothing like Alyx. It took him a moment to think of her name.

Jane Hamilton he remembered. *Her name was Jane Hamilton.*

He remembered she was fifteen and he was fourteen—four years ago. He remembered Chastity—the Sunday at the church and the looks they exchanged, but those looks—nothing came of them. Besides, Jeff had said he was going to marry her.

Alyx he thought. *I don't know if I can do this so you...*

He remembered going to Broadway with his father—remembered the man who joined them at the restaurant gouging him about not having known a woman in the biblical sense—remembered the man saying how a little want to could surprise a man the first time he did it with a woman...

Cry felt like it was the maddest piece of good-luck, as if he had gone to sea in a bowl, hoping somewhere or other to land on a white linen table cloth.

He remembered how yesterday he had stumbled on deck in the foggy dawn, the landing with the store many miles off only dawning too, a distant place he felt to be half-formed out of the chaos of the trip up river and the other half made up of his loneliness.

The phrase *making love* at once became the simple and necessary explanation of what Alyx was about.

Faster still, she moved, touching him...

"Alyx," he said aloud and then he felt the point of her blade prick his skin between his ribs...

He woke...

"You best keep to your side of the bed like you said you would," she warned.

He laughed loud and long. Alyx pricked him again with the point of the dagger and he moved against the wall, his side burning as though a honey bee had left its stinger there.

He closed his eyes and dreamed again: *cliffs five hundred feet in height rose above the boat and he, on the deck, observed bare conical hills of a place he had never visited. The hills were divided everywhere by cane-hedges into a regular checker-work of vegetation. As he dreamed, he saw himself in New York giving his father the reins of a stallion. That Alyx was present was a mystery; the*

*glimpses of Broadway scarcely seemed to
break the spell at all.*

*Point after point they passed
became great shoulders of volcanic
mountain thrust out to meet the Atlantic,
with steep green ravines furrowed in
between them that he recognized as
Virginia; and when at last they rounded a
busy street, only white walls like Moorish
towers stood before them, and a stray
sunbeam pierced the clouds on the great
mountain running out toward the bay, and
a steamship in the harbor flung out bags of
food and starving men ran to carry away
the burlap bags.*

*The women they passed were not
remarkably beautiful, but Alyx, her
complexion like rose-petals, and face soft,
shy, and innocent, was beautiful. Her
figure was one of wonder, the figure of
woman as she was meant to be, beautiful
in superb vigor, not diseased and certainly
not scarred anymore. She was erect and
strong and stately; every muscle fresh and
alive.*

He woke. Listening to Alyx breathe,
feeling the way he imagined a poet must
feel when the deepest depths inside him
have no tongue. He found himself to be
less like a poet and more like the
Cumberland, which finds expression only
on its shoals and rocks; the great heart of
it having no voice, except in its flow.

Chapter 16

"I'm sorry," he said as Alyx got out of bed. She put the dagger on the Chippendale wing chair, similar to one his mother owned but much worse for wear. She picked up her dress.

She turned to face him.

"You meant to go back on your word," she said, disappointment etched in your face.

"No, Alyx," he said. "I was dreaming that you were on top of me..."

"You should be..."

"I am ashamed," he interrupted. "And I am truly sorry."

She shook her head, slow movements left to right...

"It's the truth," he said. "Tell me a story".

"Man from Warren County bought me at the sale. I don't know who bought my sisters or my mother. I clawed his face like a panther would have when he took me away. He took me to his house, then downstairs, and chained me to the wall, facing it. Then he whipped me with a bullwhip, cutting my dress to shreds and my back until I fainted. When I came to, four men were holding me down on the dirt floor. Three, four, five more, I didn't see were rubbing salt in my wounds so they would puff up in those ugly scars

you've seen. After that they took turns
having their way with me until I wanted to
die. Memaw's dagger was in the buggy in a
burlap bag no one had looked through.
When I got to it the next day, I put on the
only other dress I had."

She stopped speaking. Cry did not
know what look he had on his face, but
her eyes were glued to his...

"Is yo got hunger, massa?" she
asked.

"No," he said, "but I'll go get
breakfast."

"Is yo uh liar, massa?"

"No, Alyx," he said. "I'm not. In the
dream, you were on top of me. That's why
I laughed. Don't you remember me doing
that?"

"I do," she said. "We'll get to that
stop I told you about today."

"I'm buying you a dress," he said,
"and a gown, shoes, and other things you
need..."

"Massa gwin ta slick me up so's Ise
fetch bigga moneys?"

"I'll never rape you, Alyx, but how
can you expect me not to feel like a man
when you're so damned beautiful?" he
asked, leaving the room before she could
answer.

Chapter 17

"How tall are you?" Cry asked Alyx from the doorway as he heard the boat's whistle, announcing its arrival in the Butler's Landing Community. The captain had told him, when he asked, where the Obey and Cumberland rivers came together and he remembered the name of the landing. He was almost ready to get off, but he had returned to get some answers from Alyx.

"I'm five foot six," she said. "Not tall at all..."

"How tall would you like to be?"

She answered, "Five foot eight."

"How much do you weigh?"

"I guess I weigh about one hundred eighteen, but I'd like to weigh more," she said.

"No," he said and she looked at him with a look he had not seen on her face before...

"I'd like to weigh a hundred thirty-five," she said.

"That would be too much, don't you think?" he asked.

"Everybody in my family was bigger than me. I'd have two more inches to spread the weight over."

"But," he said, holding his elbows against his side with his hands toward her as though he were measuring her hips. "You can't mean that..."

"It's what I want to be," she replied.

"I'll be back," he said, walking toward the door.

He followed a group of sixteen passengers and deck hands from the dock up the hill toward a row of buildings. Six men, arms loaded with items—ticking for feather or straw pillows and mattresses, shoes, large sacks of flour, coffee and sugar—passed them going down the hill to board the boat. He turned and saw Alyx and the cook on the gang plank.

She won't be there when I get back he thought but he turned his back on the women and the boat and walked quickly toward the largest building that he took to be the store.

When he opened the door and stepped over the threshold, a woman behind a long counter smiled at him.

"Welcome, young man," she called out to him. "My name is Mary. If there's anything I can help you with, just let me know."

"There is," he said, crossing the room to say in a soft voice, "I need a dress, shoes and everything a woman wears..."

"Such a red face," Mary laughed. "You're new at this..."

"First time," he said.

"Is your lady friend with you?"

"On the boat," he said.

"Is this a surprise?"

"I want it to be," he said.

"Do you know her sizes?"

64

Cry told her Alyx's height and weight, but he realized that he did not know her shoe size and told her so...

"I think we can manage," she said. "Come with me."

Cry followed her to the end of the counter and watched as she began to find items and put them behind him on the counter. She did not say anything as she gathered things he had not considered— not even imagined.

When she came toward him with outer wear, she said, "This is a most fashionable street dress for winter, made of heavy brocaded silk with three-quarter full sleeves trimmed with lace that falls to the wrist. The collar, embroidered muslin and ruffles, will please her. You should also buy this pelisse. It is a long outer garment to be worn over the dress. The pelisse is made of velvet lined with silk, and is as fashionable as any worn in Paris."

"Kentucky?" he asked.

"France, sir," she laughed. "You should also buy her at least two of these bonnets made of silk and velvet."

"I'll take everything and a gown," he said.

"We call them night shirts. She is a lucky woman," Mary said as she hurried behind the counter and began to calculate his bill. "These are duds I ordered for a woman who came in here before winter set in. Said she was a piano player—a singer on a pleasure boat. She paid me up front."

"Then you're the lucky one," Cry said. "You get paid double. Wouldn't you like to do that every day?"

"Not if she was that woman whose body they found in ice up near Burkesville or the one they found on the Natchez Trace. Men you met going down as you came up walked up the Trace from New Orleans. They know how to deal with the riff raff that preys on honest folks, unsuspecting one that start along that five hundred mile trail. No, son, I didn't double on them things... I cut you a good deal to get them outa here. Is there anything else I can get you?"

"No, ma'am," said. "You have a great day."

"You, too, young man," she smiled. "You get back this way, let me know how she likes her presents."

"I will if I do," he said, gathering his purchases.

"Since you paid in gold," the woman said, "I put a little something in your lady will appreciate."

Chapter 18

"Cry!" the captain called. "Take a minute and walk with me. You know I know the woman ain't your sister. What I don't know though is whether you understand that early Tennessee laws prescribe a penalty of $500 fine for selling a free person of color. A free person imported and sold as a slave under the law stands to recover double the price of his or her sale from the seller, who can be held until he gives bond."

"I didn't know that," Cry said, thinking *Maybe that is why Deck looked scared when I tried to give Alyx to him.*

"If that sounds like this state holds a high degree of feeling of justice toward the freeman," the captain said, "it's not that simple. I never heard of a slave ever obtaining actual justice because of that law."

"Why are you telling me this?" Cry asked.

"When I saw you coming up the plank with those fancy clothes, I thought to myself that you might be going to go after that money."

"No, sir," Cry said. "I would have stayed in Nashville if that were the case.

How do you know she was a free woman sold a slave?"

"I keep my ears open," the captain said.

"Your cook told you, didn't she?"

"No," the captain said. "When I told you I haul anything up and down this river, I meant everything. I hauled your horse and the gal down this river on the main deck below with the other slaves. I never expected I'd be taking the gal and the horse up again—ever..."

"She told me you did. She stood out from the others, didn't she?"

"She did," he answered. "But she was just cargo, nothing more. Are you a trouble maker?"

"I just want to get to Port Isabel," Cry said. "That's all..."

"A word to the wise..."

"You didn't stop me to give me a history lesson, did you?"

"Yes and no," the captain said. "I don't care what you do to the woman. That's why I put you where I did. I've got some women folk on here watching you pick up plates and they're asking who your companion is. If they see her in those clothes, it won't make a difference..."

"A difference?" Cry asked. "What do you mean?"

"I mean they'll see right through her."

"You mean they'll call her..."

"Negro's what they'll see," the captain spoke. "She may look white, but she's been a slave too long to ever be anything else in these parts. Now up where you're from it might be different, but here that's the way it is. One drop of blood in her veins is all it takes to make her a Negro."

"And these women do not believe that clothes make a person?" Cry asked.

"Clothes, nor brown hair, nor green eyes," the captain said.

"Do you have a needle?"

"Do you need to mend what you've only just bought?" the captain asked.

"No," Cry said. "I thought we'd go up and prick her finger, sir. Let that one drop of blood run out..."

"Hell, son, we can cut her damned throat and it won't spurt out!" the captain shouted. "Don't get on your high horse with me! I'll throw you and your gal over the top rail and keep your stallion for my trouble."

"What kind of women have so much power?" Cry asked.

"Women of rich and powerful men, son. Men who keep gals like yours on the side. That's the kind of women who're in the ladies quarter. That why your gal couldn't be there. Money got her a room. I was about to bed her below. Your gold did it. You understand the power of money. Now get your ass up those stairs and keep those clothes off that gal until we dock at Port Isabel."

"She won't wear the clothes outside the room," Cry said.

"I'm glad you understand," the captain said. "I wish I could get you there faster, son, but..."

I don't understand Cry thought not hearing the man's final words. *I can't even begin to imagine what it would be like to be Alyx.*

Chapter 19

The look on Alyx's face when he
knocked and she opened the door was one
he was hard pressed to interpret. He
decided it was a look more of disbelief
than of anything. He handed her
everything except the small bottle of lotion
that Mary threw in as a bonus for Alyx.

Cry closed the door and walked to
the chair. As he sat, Alyx took off her
cotton dress; tossed everything but the
new dress on the bed and kept her back
toward him as she put her arms through
the sleeves and slipped the dress over her
body.

Cry looked at her, trying not to be
obvious, but aroused, thinking *what am I
to do. She is so beautiful—married women
I've been told don't exhibit their bodies like
this.*

"Don't say massa to me," he said.

"Thank you," she said, turning to
face him. "I've never had anything like
this. I can't wear it though..."

Cry could not believe that she was
saying the only words she could have

uttered that could keep him from telling her about the captain's order...

"It's not for you to wear on this boat or on the horse when we get to Port Isabel. It is for you to wear when you get to Berea. There will be occasions when you will need it. The people who run that school must see you in it. I will buy you clothes farther up river..."

"Men's clothes," she interrupted.

"Is that what you want?" he asked.

"It will be easier for me to ride behind you in trousers," she said.

"Then I will buy you trousers and me some new ones as well when we get to another landing with a store."

"Men's shoes, too... And a shirt," she added. "I'll need one..."

"I don't think I'll buy you one of those," he laughed.

She looked at him and to his surprise, she smiled.

"Tell me a story," he said.

"The old man followed me from Lexington..."

"Deck?" Cry asked.

"Yes," she answered. "He got off the boat and went to tell the man who bought me about the horse and they came to the wharf together when we were unloaded. The man who bought me gave the old man three gold pieces and said he would buy everything, everyone of us before the sale began in order to get the horse. He did not want anyone to see the horse. He wanted the other slaves for men he knows, but he did not want me. I figure he had to decide something different for me when he saw my scars. A slave with scars is damaged goods is what he told the old man."

"Why was Deck afraid of you?" Cry asked.

"Annie told him..."

"Who is Annie?" he asked.

"The cook on this boat," she said. "She told him I had a yadicone. He once owned a slave woman with such an evil spirit in her. She killed his wife, his son, and his daughter when he went sailing. When he returned, how much later I don't know, he found the bodies. He never found the slave woman. He would have killed me if you had given me to him..."

"Or you would have killed him first," Cry said.

"I would have tried," she said, taking off her dress.

He opened the bottle of lotion while she folded the dress.

"I want to put this on your back," he said.

"Don't touch me!"

"For your scars," he said, putting the lid back on the bottle and holding it toward her as she turned around.

He closed his eyes—not because the look in her eyes scared him, but because he could not control where his eyes went.

I wish I could paint you he said to himself.

Chapter 20

During the night, Cry woke. He woke, not wanting to for he was dreaming. In his dream, his grandfather, his father's father, not German born, but literate in German and one who spoke it with his family was telling a story Cry had heard many times.

The story told why there were children in the Kreider family with the same name. Hans died at birth. The next child, a boy, was called Hans. Anna died at birth. The next child, a girl, was called Anna. Before his grandfather, Martin Kreider, died, he could never give a reason for that naming practice. Annie had clarified it for him.

Cry had tried to keep dreaming, knowing he was waking, for he wanted his grandfather to say the children were given the dead one's name so the previous child could live in the new infant. He wanted his grandfather to say that the dead child's spirit would be appeased—that the yadicone would not become an evil spirit in the mother or the child born after...

He wanted to hear his grandfather say: *In Virginia the Kreider family had slaves to help raise tobacco. In Maryland the Kreider family had slaves.*

Cry woke and remembered his grandfather's stories about the Kreiders. What he had wanted to hear his grandfather say was simply that the slaves his family owned had told the story of the yadicone and the story had influenced his grandmother or him in choosing names each time a child of the same sex was born after a previous child died at birth.

When the Kreiders moved to New York, they freed their slaves. He knew that story. When he got home, he would ask his father if he knew why his living uncles and aunts had the same names as his dead ones. He would ask him if he knew what a yadicone was...

Cry fell asleep and dreamed again, but the dream was not about dead boys and living boys—dead girls and living girls with the same name. In his dream, his grandfather spoke German but the words were English: *In the old country, it was said that there is something divine in a beautiful woman. The best of all that God is can be seen in a beautiful face.*

Cry knew he was waking, but he wanted to hold fast the dream. His grandfather, seated in his mother's heirloom chair, was pointing toward the woman behind him, standing over him. The woman was Alyx...

"Tell me your dreams," Alyx said.

Cry realized that Alyx was not talking in his dream.

"Why do you tempt me?" Cry asked.

Alyx did not answer.

"I bought you a gown," he said. "You do not wear it. You lie there naked with your grandmother's dagger in you hand and always your back toward me. In my dream, my grandfather, dead but a year now, a year this very morning, showed me how beautiful you are. If you do not want me to desire you—dream about you—wear the gown or is it that you want me to dream so that I must touch you and reach out toward you in my sleep and caress you so you can sink your dagger into my heart?"

"Here... I'll give you what I hold," she said, lifting her left arm toward him in the dark room. "Take it!"

Cry lifted his left arm, hesitating, touching her inner forearm, struck by the warmth, the softness of her skin, hesitating to take hold of her hand, but doing so. Her hand was balled. There was no dagger in it. He folded his fingers around her fist and she dropped the bottle of lotion into them.

Chapter 21

Delays on the stretch of the Cumberland River from Martinsburg to Burkesville were such that the trip would extend an extra day. Cry was on the boiler deck when the whistle blew as the steamboat prepared to dock for the night. He had not talked with the captain since they left Butler's Landing. He had not avoided the man nor sought him out.

He went to the cargo deck and fed Forrest. While he watched the horse eat, he thought about his father's passion for horse racing.

I was at the North/South race on Long Island in 1845 his story always began. The number of spectators was never the same when he told how he won two thousand dollars that day. Sometimes the number would be as few as fifty thousand, and on one occasion after he had spent the afternoon at the tavern, one hundred thousand men, women, and children had watched the horses run.

Cry decided to ride Forrest himself when the boat tied up at the dock. The cook had told him that with any luck, the boat would stop at Bakerton and Albany Landing in the morning then proceed to Creelsboro where most of the cargo would be off loaded. Before another nightfall, he should be getting off the boat at Port Isabel. She had talked quickly, smiling at him all the while.

When the horse finished eating, Cry did not water him. He would let him drink from the river which was finally flowing clear. He put the bridle on the stallion but did not take him out of the stall until the passengers and the cargo, destined for Burkesville merchants and citizens of the small town, had cleared the deck.

The stallion was calm as he led him toward the short gang plank that rested with one end on the boat and the other roped to the dock. The stallion followed him down the ramp, but stopped on the dock to snort, having smelled water. Cry led Forrest to the river's edge.

The horse drank the cold water from the river, his upper lip quivering on the surface.

"Finished, boy?" he asked the horse.

As though to say he was not, the animal lowered his head and drank deeply. When he had finished, he raised it again and drops of water fell from his mouth to the river.

The stallion followed him up the riverbank then stopped, shaking his skin and resisting Cry's pull on the lead rope. Cry knew what the horse wanted to do. He wanted to wallow. Cry saw the perfect spot some ten yards distant, but Forrest would not follow.

I'm not going to unbridle you," Cry said.

The wild look in the stallion's eyes did not unnerve Cry. He stepped toward the horse, giving only enough slack to let the horse decide what he would do. Forrest turned his head toward the left and stepped toward the side of the road. Cry worked his way around the stallion and gave the horse more slack. Forrest got down on the ground quickly, lying on his left side, whipping his tail between his legs onto his underbelly as he turned on his back. Not until the horse had worked himself upright; dropped down to complete the same ritual on his right side and back; and taken to his feet again did Cry tighten the lead rope.

Cry looked into the stallion's eyes. There was no longer any threat evident in them. Cry fastened the lead rope to the opposite side of the bridle and mounted. It had been at least a year since he had ridden bareback. The horse was ready to run.

Chapter 22

When Cry went to the dining area to get two plates, a crowd of men were gathered around a table where four men sat. One of the men spoke, his voice boisterous...

"The madman Brown, and his crazy crew, endangering the lives and property of innocent people with his insane plot," the man said, "got what he deserved. But who made Brown set sail on a course that would get his sons murdered? Who taught that crazy crew of his to band together with arms in their hands and go to Harper's Ferry? I'll tell you who... The Border Ruffians of Kansas and the Democratic Administration at Washington are the ones to blame!"

Annie brought two plates to Cry, her eyes telling him she was frightened by the men's talk.

"There is a classic fable I love to read, for it relates that any man who goes out and sows dragon's teeth will wake to find himself surrounded by a crop of armed men. This Administration has been sowing dragon's teeth for seven years. They have encouraged lawlessness and violence. They have been hurrying one locality after another toward anarchy..."

"So what can we do?" one of the men in the circle asked.

"The only sure, speedy and permanent cure is the peaceful transfer of power, at the next election. We've got to take the reins of Government—rip them from the imbecile hands that hold them—and put them into the grasp of men who neither deal in mob violence nor want to take away our rights, our property."

Cry picked up a plate in each hand and turned to leave.

"Young man," a voice called.

Cry took three steps toward the door before a hand on his shoulder almost made him spill the food from his left hand.

"Don't you have any manners?" the man who had stopped him asked.

Cry turned. No one was seated at the table. He tried to count the number of men who stood within a foot or less of where he and the other man were. He stopped trying to count and addressed the man's question.

"I'm sorry," Cry said. "I did not realize that I am the only young man in this assembly."

There was a muffled snicker and then silence...

"What do you think?" the man, the spokesman from the table, asked.

"I don't know of what you speak," Cry said.

"John Brown," the man said. "Being from the north as you are, what do you think about Harper's Ferry?"

"I've heard his name twice," Cry said. "Once in church and a second time from a slave trader named Bedford Forrest who came to visit me at my aunt's house in Nashville. I know nothing about Harper's Ferry. Is it upriver from here or below the Nashville Wharf?"

In the uproar of laughter that followed, Cry could feel his face turn red.

"You know Bedford, young man?" the man who faced him asked.

"Yes, sir," Cry said. "I have traded with him..."

"Fancy that," the man said. "So have I. Often... We traded horses, mules, and slaves almost a week ago. What did you trade?"

Cry studied the crowd and examined the silence before he said, " A Fancy Gal..."

"Well, well, young man," the man spoke. "I fear I may have misjudged you. Get along with you before the flies blow your food."

"Thank you, sir," Cry said, turning.

Before he had taken two steps, the man behind him asked, "What did you trade for, young man?"

"Massa, massa!" Annie cried out. "Uh stallyun, massa. Mabbe yu seed hit yisterdee..."

"I did, Annie and, young man, that is one fine animal. I know because I brought it down river with a load of slaves and mules on this very boat. Good night to you..."

"Good night, too, sir," Cry said. "Good night to every one of you."

Chapter 23

Cry woke while it was dark. He glanced at Alyx, on her right side as usual, sleeping...

"I hear you," she said.

"I'm not going to touch you," he told her. "Can't you sleep."

"No," she said.

"Bad dreams?"

"No," she said. "Bad memories... A man cannot understand. It can never happen to one."

"Rape, you mean," he said.

"Yes..."

"I've heard of it happening to young men," Cry said.

"It's not the same..."

"Rape is wrong. Whether it happens to a male or a female, it is wrong. I'm sorry it happened to you. I truly am," he said, unable to keep his inner voice quiet. *I would kill them all...*

The revelation took him by surprise. *To kill is wrong, but if I could find them, I would...*

"Have you been raped?" she asked.

"No," he said quickly.

"Something bothered you," she said. "Tell me..."

"I had this flash, a picture of you on the floor, your back bleeding, the salt being rubbed into your open wounds..."

"When I think I am free of it, that dream returns."

They were silent for a few minutes.

"I never thought I would ever want to kill someone, but in my heart I know I would shoot them like dogs," Cry said.

Alyx sobbed...

"Tell me a story," Cry said.

"I can't tell you their names," she said, "or I would."

"Give me the lotion," he said, "and I will rub it on your back."

She reached beneath the goose down pillow, remembering how it was to pluck the down of geese and make pillows for her grandmother. She raised her left arm without rolling backward and felt Cry take the bottle.

"It will not erase them," she said. "Killing them would not take away what they did or other men have done to me."

"I know," Cry said. "I don't know what else I can do..."

"I hate men," she said.

"I understand. I am a man, and I feel guilty somehow, for I can't control the burning, yearning lust for you that comes over me. I have heard that love is blind..."

"Love is not possible," she interrupted.

"I believe lust is blind, and love is invisible," he said.

She sighed deeply.

"I can only form an emotional attachment with women," she said.

"How does this feel?" he asked, thinking *I've got to ask you about that...*

"It feels like the first frost of winter," she cringed.

"I'm sorry," he said, blowing his breath on the white cream in his hands to warm it.

Chapter 24

Cry found the captain on the main deck the next morning and went directly toward him.

"You been hiding?" the captain asked.

"No," Cry said, realizing that the man knew he had been avoiding him.

"Fine morning..."

"It is," Cry agreed, looking into the river, flowing clear, green.

"Wind's turning the leaves upside-down like a woman's petticoat," the captain pointed toward the bank.

"I see that," Cry said. "Does it mean something?"

"Means rain," the captain said. "May not happen before we get you to Port Isabel, but it will rain."

"You're hoping for a good rain," Cry said.

The captain looked at Cry and smiled then said, "it will make the trip down river better, faster."

"Do they have a store at Creelsboro?"

"I like Creelsboro," the captain said. "Most of what's left on board will be offloaded there. It is a town, a small one. I don't know if it has more than a hundred folks. When I made my first stop, there were, maybe—fifty people living there."

"It's just been settled then," Cry said.

"No, son," the captain said. "Long hunters stayed there in 1770, under the Rock House..."

"Under a rock house?" Cry asked.

The captain laughed.

"It wasn't a house," Cry laughed, too.

"No, not a house," the captain said. "The Rock House is one of them—what do they call them? I can't remember the name, but it's like a bridge, a natural bridge, and a big one..."

"An arch?" Cry asked.

"Yes... That's it. Long hunters used it for shelter. It was the community's first church. Indians lived under it and buried their dead on top. Mine wasn't the first steamboat to come up this river. First boat to make it from Nashville to Port Isabel came up in 1833. I was a captain then, mostly on the Mississippi or the Ohio rivers. Ferries operated up and down this river before boats like this even thought of taking on this shallow water. If I remember right, the ferry at Creelsboro was crossing back and forth around 1814. I know you're thinking that ain't long ago compared to your city..."

"No," Cry said, "it's not that long ago, but I wasn't thinking that. I was thinking I should ask you if I'll have time to ride my horse."

"You will. And you might want to buy that gal something at the store. You know..."

"I think I know that you were protecting her by telling me the women would cause us problems. I think the slave trader is the reason you wanted her to stay in the room."

"Annie's taking care of her I hope. Empties her honey pot, I know, and sees you two get fed. If she ain't done a good job, I need to know. I may be going to Texas, but I take pride in what I do. Last run I make, I expect the crew to work its hardest. I told you what I told you for your own good and hers, too, but mostly yours."

"I need to mail a letter," Cry said. "I don't suppose they have a post office in Creelsboro, do they?"

"Yes they do, son. Creelsboro's one of the twelve top trading centers on this river. They've got a constable, a tavern if you want to wet your whistle or get some food. Then there's the store, a hotel, a Union Church. Hell, there's even a tanyard, doctors, and an academy."

"For whites only?"

"What a damned, dumb question son. Why would you ask that?"

"Alyx wants to go to school. I'm taking her to Berea where they have a school for blacks and whites, males and females..."

"Damnation, son! Talk like that is what's causing all this row about war that I'm hearing."

"War?" Cry asked.

"There's gonna be war son. Mark my words. Sure as there's gonna be rain, there'll be war. This river won't be safe for trade. Armies will be running up and down it; crossing it; shooting each other; and God only knows if this country will be one or two. God only knows. Mark my words."

Chapter 25

When Cry came out of the store, a man held Forrest's lips, one in each hand.

"He's seven," Cry said.

"Got any likker?" the man asked, his voice firm.

"No, sir," Cry said. "I sure don't have..."

"Got any wimmen?"

"No, sir," Cry said. "I'm alone out here."

"Well, I like likker and I like wimmen, but I shore do like this stud hoss. Want ta sell him?'

"He's not mine. I bought him at auction in Nashville. He's my father's. I'm taking him to New York."

The man stood erect, his shoulders, broad. His large, black eyes glittered. It was as though they were able to look through Cry. His hair, the blackest of black, very thick and cut rather short, gave him an intelligent look.

An honest farmer Cry thought.

"Ya ain't taking the hoss," the man said.

Cry raised his eyebrows, his eyelids exposing more of his eyes.

He's strong Cry thought. *He looks agile and he's in front...*

"Name's Champ Ferguson," the man said, extending his hand.

When Cry took the man's hand, his grip was firm and he applied equal pressure.

"Pleased to meet you, sir. My name's Martin Kreider."

"That filly over there iz mine, Martin Kreider" Champ said. "She iz uh fleet thing and younger than yore stud. Ya ain't taking him back ta that boat until we cross the river on Grider's ferry and race up the bottom. I come down here ta race. Man didn't show."

"Sir," Cry began...

"Champ," the man said.

"Champ, sir..."

"Jist Champ," the man said. "Don't tell me ya've got uh boat ta ketch. It ain't much unloaded. Don't tell me ya ain't got no saddle..."

"I don't have one, sir..."

"Champ..."

"Champ, I don't have a saddle..."

"I'll take mine off'n the mare if ya can't ride bareback..."

"I can ride bareback," Cry said.

Six men from the store stood on the porch, looking at the men and the horse.

"Is there gonna be a race?" one of the men asked.

"Shore 'nuf," Champ said. "We get off that ferry, Mr. Grider, I want ya ta start us. Here take my pistol."

Champ went to his mare; untied her; and led her next to Cry.

"Fetch his stuff," Champ said, pointing at the clothes Cry held. "Put 'em inside and let's do hit."

It was impossible for Cry to refuse or resist. He understood that and he felt better, his fear of the man having peaked. It took only a few minutes to load the horses and the men on the ferry and about a minute to cross the river.

Champ led his horse off first and Cry followed, thinking *my horse is more like this man than his mare is.*

"Git ya up now, Martin," Champ said. "Soon as that pistol cracks, ride like hell for I aim ta... My old hat's up the road about half a mile on the right. We turn there and end her here."

Cry mounted in one fluid leap. The gunshot followed with no other warning and the mare bolted, Champ spurring her, and Forrest followed. Cry leaned forward; loosened the reins; and rode. Champ yelled—not at his horse—yelled because he was a horseman. Cry yelled, too, as Forrest closed on the mare. At the turn, Champ, leaning down, picked up his hat and whipped it against his mare's neck. She covered the ground quicker than Cry would have dreamed she ever could. Forrest accepted her challenge, his hooves seeming not to touch down, but the sound of them beat the earth like a drum. Neck and neck at the last quarter of a mile, Champ looked at Cry and urged the mare on, but the stallion moved ahead, and finished the race two lengths in front of her.

As they walked the horses, steam rising from them like fog from the river, Champ said, "I want a yearling out of yore stud, Martin. Just bring it down ta Spring Creek tother side of Albany. Everybody can tell ya where I live. I never expected my mare ta beat yore stallion, but I expected ya ta git him beat."

"I'll do my best, Champ, but I can't make any promises where the horse is concerned. My father..."

"Would have been proud of ya and him," Champ said. "I'm not crossing the river with you. I'll get my gun from Mr. Grider then ride south. Albany lies up the bottom uh fur piece and I aim ta shoot me a deer fur supper."

Chapter 26

"Thanks for the outfit and the scissors," Alyx said when Cry turned from his left side to his back.

"The slave trader who took you to Nashville is on the boat with us," Cry said.

"Annie told me," Alyx said.

"I figured as much. Captain has been edgy the whole trip, thinking you might sue him for selling you and you a free woman..."

"I know," she said.

"Annie?"

"Yes," Alyx said.

"Tell me a story, Alyx..."

"I can't think of anything else to tell you, Cry," she said.

"Tell me how you ended up in Paris, Kentucky," Cry suggested.

Alyx did not say anything.

"I won a race today," Cry said.

"I heard. Some things you might not want to hear," she whispered.

"That could be," he said. "I've been hearing men talk of war and a man named John Brown. I've been hearing men talk about slavery, abolitionists, and I haven't wanted to hear those things," he said.

"They say our ancestors were nothing short of animals," she said. "Say slavery gives us a way to contribute... Say maybe in another hundred years we can be free. It ain't so."

"I'm glad I got you... That's not how I wanted to say that. I'm glad you came up river with me."

"Why?" she asked.

"I can't tell you. It's not a secret," he said.

"Don't tell me," she said. "I don't want to hear it."

"I can't talk to my horse either," Cry laughed.

Alyx snickered.

"After they raped me, they left me naked and I cried. I had so many pains, but the pain in my heart was the worst. When the house got quiet, I went out to the barn and got my bag; put on my dress—it soaking up the bloody brine—and I found the Green River—not knowing for sure it was the Green, but knowing, even in the dark, I had to travel up stream."

"So you went home?"

"I went to an empty house," she said. "It took me two weeks of hiding and eating things I'd never eaten, but in that first daylight, I knew it was the Green River. It smelled the same. It flowed the same and I followed it. And I got home, but it wasn't home. A man and a woman who had bought it came the day after I got there. They found me. The man wanted to keep me. The woman touched my cheek. She told him they would keep me. They built a hiding place for me under the stairs by closing in the steps. There was a small door that opened out and a trap door inside that led down into the walled up cellar. The outside door was always open in case I needed to get inside and down in a hurry. I could bar the trap door from below and hide in the cellar like a rat if anyone came looking for me. "

"And they found you?" Cry asked.

"No," she said. "They came often that first year, but after that I never had to hide. The man's name was John and the woman's name was Sarah. I never knew their last names. We worked the fields and one day John began to chop down a forked hickory tree just past the barn. Sara wanted an orchard so John chopped each day. One morning he went out to finish the job, so he said, while we washed the dishes. We heard the crash when the tree fell and Sara dropped the plate she was drying. She had a premonition that John was under the tree. He was. Sara and I tried to chop the tree below his feet and above his head, but we couldn't get him out. Sara rode one of the mules to the nearest neighbor's farm and came back with three men. I knew them. They knew me. One of them cussed John, saying *a forked tree is too dangerous for a man to cut—no one can tell which way it will fall.*"

"One of the men betrayed you," Cry said.

"I told Sarah he would. After we buried him, she put me on the other mule and told me to follow the river. I got all the way to Tebbs Bend before they caught me," she said.

She stopped talking. She let him reach out to her and hold her while she cried.

Chapter 27

"Tell me how you got to Paris," Cry said.

"Man from Warren County was with the men who caught me at Tebbs Bend," she said. "He took me to Louisville where he said he'd sell me down south for the cotton fields. Woman bought me there and took me to Paris."

"Did she free you?"

"She hired me out," Alyx said. "I worked at the tavern. It was a beautiful stone building; two and a half story with a high basement and attic. It had a gate of wrought iron with a spread eagle on the north side. I often dreamed that I was an eagle and in that dream I always flew to Canada. I bought my freedom from her."

"How long did it take you?"

"Too long," she answered. "She didn't mean for me to ever manage it. I earned three dollars a month at the tavern. I gave it all to her. After two years, I asked her how much longer until I'd be free. She told me seven years—maybe ten. I decided if I meant to be free I'd have to do anything for money. Men at the tavern kept asking me to go up to their rooms with them. I started doing that, but I couldn't stand their hands on my body. I got good at doing things they wanted without letting them do anything to me. One day a Frenchman came to town. He asked me if I would model for him; paid me to take off my clothes; he never tried anything with me—just told me how to sit or stand; recline; lie on the bed. He asked me if maybe I could find another girl and I thought he was through with me. I asked him what I was doing wrong. *Wrong?* he asked me in his strange accent. *You do good. You with another girl* he smiled."

Alyx stopped speaking. Cry looked into her eyes. She did not close them nor look away. She looked and Cry knew she wanted him to ask her something, but he didn't know what to ask...

"There was another girl—in the kitchen. I asked her. She was hired out like me. We went up to his room. He told us about Sappho, a woman from ancient Greece. She lived on the island of Lesbos, wrote poems about love between women. He said in ancient Sparta women loved women. He talked about harem women in Arabia and a Caliph who had two women beheaded for lovemaking. He told us about love between men and boys and winked at us. He painted us night after night. He wanted us to do things to each other. I would do things to her, but I would never let her do things to me. When he left, we worked together. A man would ask me or her to go up to his room, and we would only go if he would take us both. That's how I bought my freedom in one more year."

"I bet the woman who bought you was surprised," Cry said.

"She was furious," Alyx said. "I thought she wasn't going to let me go, but she did. She said she could buy another girl like me any day when she went with me to get my paper. Getting that paper was the best feeling I've ever had in my life. I kept working at the tavern. It was the stopping place for the stagecoach. With twenty rooms, a billiard room, and a ballroom, there were always men and whisky. One night, a man told me about Berea. He'd been there and was headed back to Maysville. He told me Berea had a one-room school, but it would be a college soon. I decided I would go to Berea when the stage came back through. I was on my way to work for the last time when I was kidnapped."

"With any luck," Cry said. "you'll be in Berea tomorrow night."

Chapter 28

"Which way do we go on this cold, muddy road?" Cry asked when they got to Mt. Vernon.

"Left," Alyx said. "They called this the Wilderness Road when they drove us along it and through here at night on the way to Port Isabel. The chains around the men's legs woke the people in that white house up there. A man came out in his night shirt with a lamp in his hand. We camped outside town a mile or more toward a place they called Crab Orchard."

"So Berea's not far from here?"

"Not as far on Forrest," she said, "as it was on foot."

Cry smiled when she called the horse by his name.

"Tell me..."

"No more stories," Alyx laughed.

"Believe it or not," he said, " I was going to say: tell me why you wanted the scissors."

"To cut my hair," she answered.

"I like it the way it is," Cry said.

"Do you like the way I'm dressed?"

"You never liked the dress, did you?" he asked.

"I loved it. It was so sweet of you to buy it, but I couldn't wear it..."

"Was it too big? The woman who sold it to me said it should fit."

"It was perfect," she said.

"You tried it on again?"

"The day you raced," she said.

"And you never let me see you in it? I'm mad..."

"No, you're not," she said.

"How do you know I'm not angry?"

"You care for me," she said, hugging him and laughing.

"Why do you say that?"

"You kept your word," she said.

"It was hard," he said. "You have to know that."

She hugged him tighter, pulling him back toward her.

"You left it on the boat," he said.

"Yes..."

"Why?"

"Because I couldn't bring it with me..."

"I don't see why not..."

"Because I'm going to be a man," she said.

"Why would you say that?" he asked.

"At Berea, I want to study science and explore medicine on my own," she said. "The scissors are for my hair. Just before we get to the school, I want you to cut my hair short."

"That's why you wanted the trousers," he said.

"Yes, it was..."

"What are you going to do with your breasts?" he asked.

"I don't like breasts," she said.

"I like yours," he said, feeling his face flush.

"Why?" she asked.

Cry did not answer.

"Tell me a story, Cry..."

"About breasts?"

"About why you like my breasts..."

"On the boat," he began... "When you were sleeping or sitting on the bed with your back to me, I would look at them..."

"And want to rape me?" she asked.

"I was tempted to make love to you," he said, " but I wanted to paint you, too."

"Before or after I told you about the Frenchman?"

"Before," he said. "Why don't you like breasts?"

"I like being comfortable," she said.

"I feel them against my back," he said although the jacket she wore kept him from feeling them.

She took her arms from around his body and pushed him forward. Forrest answered his lunge with a burst of speed that almost caused her to fall off and under him. She grabbed Cry again and squeezed him as she gripped the horse with her legs.

"I like your legs, too," Cry laughed, reining in Forrest.

"Right now, I like them just fine, too," she said. "I'll bind my breasts and I won't hug men."

"You'll have to lust after women," Cry said.

"I can do that," she said.

"And learn to cuss..."

"And drink whisky," she laughed.

"Walk with a swagger...Chaw bakker..."

"And spit..."

"I've got a better idea," Cry said.

"What's that?"

"Go home with me and Forrest," Cry whispered.

Chapter 29

When Cry cut the first stands of hair, he took the book that Deck had given him from the inside pocket of his coat. He opened the book with his right hand, holding it and the scissors while he placed the two inch lock inside. He put the book back into the pocket and looked at Alyx.

"You sure you want me to do this?" he asked.

"I'm sure," she said.

He began to cut long strands of her hair, shaking his head slowly left to right, cutting more and more as he tried to achieve as good a man's cut as he was able.

"Do you feel you strength fading?" he asked.

"I know that story," she answered. "No..."

"Proves you're not a man," he laughed.

"Do you get weak when you get your hair cut?"

"I always think about Samson when I get it cut," he said. "When I was younger, four or five, I'd cry."

"Is that how you got your nickname?" she asked.

"Yes," he said, pursing his lips.

"Someone's coming!" Alyx exclaimed.

Cry heard the unmistakable sound of a horse's hooves, running full speed in spite of the soft road. Before either he or

Alyx could mount Forrest, the other horse and rider were upon them. The rider was a young man, reining hard to stop his lathered horse, a bay, a mare almost as tall as Forrest.

"Well, well," the young man, whom Cry took to be no older than he was, said, "look at what I've found. Abolitionist, ain't ya?"

"No," Cry said.

"Got a white negra, have you?" he asked, looking at the hair on the roadside. "And uh female... Well, hell..."

"We're not looking for trouble," Cry said.

"Well, trouble's found ya," the young man said. "When I first came over here from Rockcastle County, I was eight, maybe nine... This here area was called the Glade. Weren't nothing here but a few scattered farms and uh racetrack. Three years later that sonsabitch Clay brought that preacher man Fee here to build uh church. The damned fool built uh one-room school back up there in this wilderness that me and the boys from Richmond closed down. Blacks and whites together ain't gonna happen round these parts. We own slaves. The likes of John Brown, Fee and Clay want them to revolt. I come up here to see that everybody's gone. I find ya sneaking in... Ya got to be some kind uh damned fool..."

This can't be real Cry thought.

"Now I'm taking yore slave gal and yore hoss, Mr. abolitionist missionary man," the stranger said, dismounting, pointing a pistol at the side of Cry's head. "I should just drop ya right here, right now. Git my saddle and blanket off the mare. Put it on yore hoss and maybe I'll let ya go up to that little village named after some Bible town. Stop, gal. Don't git in the way!"

Cry removed the saddle and blanket from the mare and moved between the stranger and Alyx feinting a stumble so he could drop the scissors.

"Damn ya! Watch yore step," the stranger put the pistol between Cry's eyes.

Given no quarter, Cry put the blanket on Forrest and then the saddle...

Cinch it tight, bastard...Come, gal!"

Cry looked at Alyx, but did not speak. The stranger put the pistol in his left hand and pulled Alyx up behind him.

"Fetch me them reins!" the stranger ordered.

Cry led the mare toward Forrest and the riders.

I'll hit Forrest across the rump Cry thought but he handed the reins to the stranger and watched him begin to ride away. The man turned toward his left and shot. Cry heard Alyx scream then he dropped to his knees and fell forward into the road.

Journeys

Book Two

The Wolf by the Ears

Chapter 1

"Cry?"

"Yes, General," Cry answered.

"I've called a Council of War with my commanders. We'll meet shortly. You know something?"

"What, sir?"

"I've meant to, but I've never thanked you for what you've done for me. I've so many others that I need to thank as well for what they've done."

"You owe me no thanks, sir," Cry said. "Any thanks should be going one way..."

"And how's that?"

"To you... From this army to you, sir, and from this country. The men who run it owe you more than any of them will ever admit..."

"What does a man want to receive thanks for, anyhow, Cry? I'm not ambitious and I don't have any political aspirations."

"But you would thank me..."

"That's different... A man should want to thank his friends," the General said.

"What was it that Lincoln said of you?"

"Many things, Cry. When Cump asked him why he did not nominate me to lead an army, he answered that I was born in Virginia and there were doubts as to my loyalty."

"I heard him say he stood up for you..."

"Cump did... He told me he said, Mr. President, Old Tom is as loyal as I am, and as a soldier he is superior to all on your list."

"And you are, sir. You've proved that."

"I don't have to prove anything, son," General Thomas said. "Lincoln asked Cump if he would be responsible for me... Cump said he told him he would with the greatest of pleasure."

"He knew he wouldn't have to be responsible for you," Cry said.

"I suppose he knew that then, but I sense a change in him now and in Lincoln."

"I read where Lincoln said this country can only gain peace by whipping the Rebels. He gives credit now where it's due."

General Thomas smiled. "Calls the six of us—Grant, Cump, Sheridan, Farragut, Porter, and me—his missionaries of unconditional surrender, Cry. He's impatient with me now though..."

"I think he's not so much impatient as Grant is. Grant sees you as so many saw Rosecrans, but your friend General Sherman..."

"Cump... You think Cump still willing to be responsible for me, do you?"

"I believe he understands your certainty of movement as I understand it. Tonight your commanders will tell you not to fight until you are ready."

"And what do you say, Cry?"

"I say the slippery hills around this city will thaw soon and we'll have more horses—more guns for you when you decide the time is right to make a go of it."

"Do you believe, Cry, that dreams come from the future?"

"I don't know, sir. Mine seem to come from the past. Why?"

"Because I dreamed last night that I attacked the enemy this morning and drove his army from the river below this city to a high hill," General Thomas said.

"And then what happened?" Cry asked.

"I woke up. I couldn't dream the rest of it no matter how I tried."

"I dreamed of Alyx last night."

"Has it been a while since you dreamed of her, Cry, or have you simply not mentioned her?"

"If it's possible to dream all night long about her, I do. But I've learned that it's not possible to dream her into the present."

"I must go, son, but know this: I appreciate you..."

"You don't have to," Cry said.

"Let me say it, anyway. I appreciate you for being on the side of the oppressed. Who would've thought that a wounded boy, shot through his lungs, would come to me in Kentucky, not wanting to be a soldier, and stand before me now fearless but wise?"

"I've had a great teacher, sir..."

"You give me too much credit, Cry."

"Not enough, sir," Cry said. "I've found a gun maker in Kentucky who is loyal. I must get to him before Forrest does."

"Forrest," General Thomas said. "Cump tells me I should kill him if it takes the loss of ten thousand men to do it."

"Was he on the field in your dream, sir?"

"You know, son," the General said. "I don't think he was. Get some sleep before you take off again."

"I'll try, Pap. You have a productive meeting."

"I'll talk as little as possible and listen much to what they have to say..."

Chapter 2

Cry tried to sleep, but he could not. His thoughts were ones he had mulled more times than he could count. He struggled not to close his eyes, for if he did, he knew he would revisit the scene on the muddy road outside Berea. He would see the man ride away on his horse with Alyx behind him and he would see the man turn to his left and shoot.

He lost a year of living because of that shot, but the book in his inside coat pocket, the one Old Deck had given him, saved his life, deflecting the ball of lead toward his right away from his heart and into his right lung, separating his lower ribs upon entrance and exiting from the right side of his upper body.

A Negro who had been freed by Cassius Clay to work at the sawmill in Berea found him and carried him into the deserted village; worked with him through the night, then drove him to Lexington the following morning.

It was he who saved my life he thought, but the doctor in Lexington who treated him the following day said it was the pages of the book that plugged the wound and stopped the bleeding that kept him alive.

Although he lost a year of his life, he gained a year of political education due to his incessant reading of newspapers, *The New York Herald, Harper's Weekly,*

Louisville Courier, and *Nashville Dispatch.*
He could recall many things that he had
read that Lincoln had said in his speeches
before the election. He believed many of
the man's words, especially: *Two men on a
plank—either can rightfully push the other
off!* He wanted to believe other things he
had read, like: *the north believes in the
equality of man and in believing thus
slavery is wrong.* Reading about Lincoln,
he had formed a picture of the man who
would be president. On the outside, he
projected anarchy and confusion to
appear politically correct, but on the
inside, Cry reasoned, there was a method
behind his facade. There came to mind his
words about what had been the prevailing
assumption of the time that: *unless white
man enslaves the negro, the negro will
enslave the white. In that case, I think I
would go for enslaving the black man, in
preference to being enslaved myself.*

Reading, he learned that the nation
was one sixth slave. He would not have
thought it so. One of six, men, women,
and children were property and nothing
else to their owners. He was too sick to
vote for Lincoln in the November election,
but he would have done so in spite of the
fact that most editorials foretold of war if
the man were to be elected. He
remembered Captain Millikin's words to
him when he had said that Alyx wanted to
go to Berea where there was a school for
blacks and whites. The words echoed in

his ears in the silence of the room: *Talk like that is what's causing all this row about war..."*

Of all the things he had read on the subject of slavery, the words of Thomas Jefferson stood out: *We have the wolf by the ears, and we can neither hold him nor safely let him go...*

Jefferson's words explained slavery and the nation's dilemma for him better than any other article he had read. Being with Alyx had shown him that politicians, slave owners, and people who believed in the equality of man would not profess the good qualities of slavery if they were enslaved themselves. In that regard, Lincoln had spoken for all of them.

The war came in April. He was not well in April, but knew he had to go back to Kentucky and begin his search for Forrest; his quest for Alyx.

He closed his eyes and he could see her in the darkness as he had seen her on the steamboat, her naked body with those hideous scars , her small waist and her well-toned legs.

Toward morning, he fell asleep.

Chapter 3

As he rode the train from Nashville toward Kentucky, the words of the General came back to him: *not wanting to be a soldier...* The man—he and most of the soldiers under his command called *Pap*—had taken one look at the frail boy he was when he drove his team of mules into Camp Dick Robinson in the fall of '61 and had immediately told him to go home.

The General had followed him outside and Cry thought at the time that he had done so because he wanted to make sure one so frail would leave his camp. He had never asked Pap if that were so. The mules were what had taken the General's eyes at once. He remembered the excitement in the General's voice when he had said *come back inside, boy, and let's talk a minute...*

The minute became a lengthy lesson about the state of the war in Kentucky. The General told him how there were men willing to fight, but the men had no arms, no clothing, no blankets, no tents.

And I have no mules he had said *no wagons—no drivers—no competent quartermaster staff.*

He smiled as he remembered how the General had explained his most pressing needs, for mules, for wagons, for soldiers, experienced, trained soldiers, not volunteers or recruits *barefoot and naked...*

When the General had offered to buy his new wagon for $110, his mules for $125 each, Cry had been adamant in his refusal.

The General had told him how he had been ordered to buy mules in the country where the troops were raised in the hope that it would have a beneficial effect upon the Union sentiments of the people and had even handed him the original order from Simon Cameron, Secretary of War, a short message that had been forwarded from Lieutenant Nelson.

The General had bought his team, four young, broke mules, two reds and two blacks, perfectly matched teams sixteen hands high, muscled and tall like their draft horse dams, but Cry would not take money for the wagon. For the wagon, he had demanded a horse and not just any horse, but a cavalry mount, fully equipped with scabbards for a rifle and two pistol holsters for his saddle.

Only if you've got the guns the General had said.

Cry had turned and walked out of the General's office without saying a word. Again, the General had followed closely...

From beneath the wagon seat, he had handed the General his Spencer, patented in 1860, a .52 caliber, capable of sending out seven aimed shots within thirty seconds and hitting a target at 500 yards.

From his knapsack, he had taken two Colt .44 caliber six-shot revolvers, the 1860 New Model Army which, from 16 yards could send a bullet through seven white pine boards, each 3/4" thick, even when separated by one inch of dead space between them.

Thank God he thought as the train strained to climb a steep grade *the man who shot me at Berea only had a small caliber pocket pistol...*

It was after he had taken two 1858 model Remington, the improved series of simplified revolver with a solid frame, which made the arm stronger and cheaper to produce than the Colts in either a .44 or a .36 caliber... It was at that moment that the General had said: *you're not wanting to be a soldier, son* and had told him: *I don't have the horse you need with me at this moment, but, if at all possible, I will get one here in a day or two. Bunk in my office so we can talk.*

Instead of talking, the General had folded the top half of a dispatch then had given it to him. Cry still could close his eyes, which he did, and read the words of Thomas E. Bramlette : *I can't hear from my family at Columbia. If any letters or news comes from there to me, do me the great kindness to forward it. I rest uneasy for news from my wife and little children at that place, now held, as I learn, by traitor troops.*

It was then that the General had asked: *Where did you get the guns?*

My father bought them for me he had answered.

Can you use them?

I've had a year of reading newspapers and using them as targets, sir, he had said and then he had told the story of Alyx, Forrest, and Berea.

The General had given him another dispatch to read in its entirety. He could still remember the part of it that pertained to him, the words he pictured clearly were: *The postmaster here informs me that there is a large amount of mail matter in the office here for your command. He says if you will send in some properly authorized person the mails will be turned over to him, put up in packages for the different regiments.*

Cry was ashamed of what he had said to General Thomas that day: *With all due respect, sir, I don't have time to be an errand boy.*

You've got to learn to slow down, son, the General had said, telling him: *When I was a boy I gave the slaves on our farm bible and reading lessons. While I was stationed in Florida I conducted botanical studies. While I was stationed at Ft. Yuma I conducted zoological studies which were praised by experts. While I was stationed at Ft Yuma I compiled a 70-word dictionary of a local Indian language, a work praised by ethnologists. I was wounded by an arrow through the flesh of my chin that went into my chest during a skirmish with Comanche just this year in Texas. I pulled it out and went back to work. I learned something from their tactics. You can't go rushing off on your own personal war to get back a woman and a horse. I want you to help me and I'll help you do everything I can to win your little war. I need you to go to Louisville and bring back the mail. If Bramlette has mail, I want you to take it to him at Camp Nelson. I'll have a man give you directions. You need to know who these men are, Cump and Bramlette, and I want them to know who you are. Do you think your father can find me some guns?*

Money talks Cry remembered he had answered.

I'll get the money the General had said *and you'll be the one to take it to him.*

Chapter 4

As the train approached his stop, Cry was glad he had met Sherman and Bramlette. Meeting them had helped him understand their motives, particularly their political ambitions. General Sherman was on his march toward the sea, set upon destroying the south in a new way, taking with him the veteran troops that had composed the Army of the Cumberland under General Thomas.

With Sherman, there was a man named Richard Hibberd, a native of England who came to America in 1863 and enlisted in the 147th Illinois, assigned as part of the Army of the Cumberland under General Thomas. Working together, they learned...

I like what we do for Pap Cry could hear Dick saying at Chickamauga when the two of them left the parapets to go for ammunition while Longstreet's men made another desperate charge.

He hoped his messenger had gotten through to Dick Hibberd, for Dick would gather what guns and horses he could for Pap's cavalry without Sherman's approval or knowledge. Impressing horses, guns and ammunitions for Pap was one of the many things the two of them had done successfully before General Sherman came on the scene.

When General Thomas authorized the issue of provisions to the suffering people his army encountered during the hundred days from Dalton to Atlanta, General Sherman found out about it and fumed. It was soon afterwards that he had split them, taking Dick with him, because he could—Dick being enlisted—*leaving me with Pap because I would not be subordinate.* Sherman had shouted: *no more!* to Thomas, not only about the food, but about Pap's style of warfare. Cry had stood in hearing distance of the two men when Sherman had ordered Pap to *get back to wagons and marching. An army on the move has no need for regular headquarters in camp or that circus wagon of yours... that office...*

When Sherman began his march to the sea with 62,000 fully equipped veterans and a larger cavalry than he left behind, he marched away from the central theater of war.

Cry Pap had said to him when he learned that what he feared would happen had begun to fall into place—that Hood, newly appointed by President Davis, with a veteran army that had resisted both him and Sherman, was moving toward Nashville...

Cry Pap had said to him: *I can't see the merit in attacking railroads and burning towns the way Cump explained it to me as he carefully inspected my men and equipment after Atlanta...*

Leaving you every weak man, the wounded and sick, 15,000 whose service was ending—who are now gone— and giving you orders to defend Nashville Cry had answered, *damn him to hell!*

I asked for my old corps Pap had said...

I know...

My entire equipment of trains, pontoons—my essentials...

He took...

Let's not forget the contrabands Cump despised Pap had smiled, referring to the Negroes who had followed them from Atlanta and had formed a procession behind Sherman's troops.

You know why, don't you?

Advise me Pap had smiled again.

Cump has sent a dispatch to Grant congratulating him for being next in line to be President...

You think so?

It is a fact Cry had stated.

Grant has advised me to fight Hood, pressed me to fight, ordered me to fight, threatened me with removal if I do not fight...

To cover his damned ass for letting Sherman march!

What else have you learned?

Secretary Stanton is in a panic. He fears if you wait for Wilson to get ready, Gabriel will be blowing his last horn...

Does it appear to you that their dreams are dreaming us?

No, sir, it does not...

How does it appear to you?

That I have to get to Louisville and bring back the dismounted men you sent there for horses and arms...

At least the arms, Cry, and we will have a go at this...

The passenger car rattled and Cry remembered the first time he took the mail to Bramlette, now Governor of Kentucky. He learned that the man had grown up as a neighbor of Champ Ferguson. As boys, they had fought along the banks of Spring Creek. As men, they were enemies. Bramlette, a staunch supporter of Lincoln when the war began was now the man's most outspoken critic. Lincoln's Proclamation and his call for Negro troops had made them political enemies. Champ had declared his own war upon Union men he called Lincolnites...

In the beginning, besides carrying mail and messages, Cry had been called upon to drive the mules and the wagon he had sold to the General. On one occasion, he met two wagonloads of supplies in Nicholasville that were sent by Bramlette. He had been sent by General Thomas to take charge of them and escort them to Camp Dick Robinson. Each return trip from Bramlette's camp gave Cry the opportunity to stop in Richmond or Mt. Vernon and ask about his horse and a young woman dressed like a man. No return trip or foray into the ghostlike village of Berea turned up any information. He quickly learned that information was guarded by those who supported the Union and those who opposed it...

Providing food for soldiers was the business of the Commissary of Subsistence department. When General Thomas marched to Lebanon to guard the railroad there, he ordered Cry to report to Christopher Beeler, the commissary, to help issue a daily ration of pork or bacon, fresh or salt beef, and eighteen ounces of flour. It was he who hauled potatoes, peas, beans and rice, coffee or tea, sugar, vinegar, salt, pepper, candles, and soap from the depot to the commissary building.

Pap had told him how he got his start in the mess when he was sent to Florida after West Point. The General had told him he learned how to value supplies when they had none in the garrison. In the Mexican War, his artillery had battled under constant fire early morning until afternoon.

"I don't teach target practice with pistols," the General had said one morning, picking up three potatoes from the pile that Cry had been peeling and walking to the door of the commissary. "Come."

Cry had followed him into the street.

"Let's see what you can do with this," Pap said tossing one partially peeled potato into the air.

Cry drew, fired, shattering the potato.

"Now," Pap shouted, tossing the other two potatoes.

Cry shot first one potato and then the other.

"Can you shoot like that with your left hand?"

"I can," Cry assured him.

"I think it's time I get you out of the commissary," Pap said.

While he was in Lebanon, Cry met Colonel Frank Lane Wolford, an Adair County native who organized the 1st Kentucky Cavalry. Cry saw at once that his men displayed little of the drill and discipline that General Thomas demanded of his soldiers, but he also saw that the cavalry was made up of men who had the utmost confidence in Wolford and he in them. They had received their baptism by fire at the Battles of Wildcat Mountain, turning Zollicoffer's army toward the Cumberland Gap and into the mountains of East Tennessee. Like Brammlette, Wolford protested the use of Negro troops. Rather than cease doing so as he had been advised, Wolford resigned.

As the train slowed to a stop at Franklin, Kentucky, Cry got up and began to make his way toward the exit. He would have only a short time to make contact

with his cousin, Jeff, and give him money
for the repeating rifles that would be
bought from the local gunsmith. He had
not seen Jeff in more than two months nor
his aunt and uncle since they moved from
Nashville to New York. He saw Chastity
and her parents on the day they migrated
to Clay County, Missouri.

"Cry!" Jeff shouted from the depot.

Cry rushed toward his cousin. They
stopped within a couple of feet of each
other, saying nothing except with their
eyes.

Cry broke the silence, asking, "How
is everyone?"

"Good," Jeff said. "Actually better
than good. New York is far from the war."

"Have you heard from Chastity?"

"They're having it rough. Missouri is
a lawless border state. I wish I had
married her. She would've loved New
York..."

"If not for the Yankees?" Cry asked.

"Yes," Jeff laughed. "Uncle Martin
will meet you in Louisville."

"What's wrong?"

"He said he has to talk to you. I
don't know any more than that."

"You've almost lost your Tennessee
drawl," Cry said.

"And you've taken it up," Jeff
laughed again. "I got word to Old Red Fox
Ellis like you asked me to and finally
found Tinker Dave where you said he'd be
in that cave of his..."

"What did they say?"

"They'll have fresh horses for General Thomas by the time you get back from Louisville. They've reached out to Unionists in North Carolina and Georgia for horses if Sherman ain't taken them for his army. There are horses waiting for you in Louisville. Horses are due today from Missouri, Arkansas, and Ohio and I don't know where else you have contacts. Your man in Washington sent word that Grant meant to replace Thomas first with Schofield then with Logan, but now he plans on going to Washington then coming to Nashville to take command himself."

"Damn him to hell, anyway!"

"Give me the money and I'll get on my way. I don't know how many guns Uncle Martin has, but he said a few thousand. Will Thomas be able to handle Hood?"

"Hood was defeated at Franklin. He's wasted his army. I saw a Reb general and his horse, both dead on the Union breastworks, him hanging down the horse's back. I heard that Cleburne, one of the South's best, died there too. He may have been the one I saw. Six generals were killed there. I believe Hood's lost the best of his commanders. He has hopes that help will come to him."

"Will it?"

"It won't," Cry said.

"Grant's saying Hood will move into Kentucky... Maybe even cross into Ohio..."

"Pap is waist deep in careful planning right now. What we get to him, he'll use to move out to meet Hood and inflict the maximum amount of damage to that army at the least cost to his own men."

"Washington talk says he's drilling Negro regiments. That's not settling well..."

"Steedman's regiment," Cry said. "They'll fight. Fully a third of Pap's army will be quartermaster's employees, garrison troops, and the Negro regiments never before committed to battle."

"What about you?" Jeff asked.

"I'll be fine," Cry said. "Hood should have retreated from Franklin. Now he can't and he can't move into Kentucky. I pity his men. Pap has learned to combine firepower and maneuvers with such a precision the likes of which Washington has never witnessed. Hood would have to have an equal or superior amount of force to win. He has neither."

"I brought you some *Harper's Weekly* to read while you ride," Jeff said.

"Good," Cry said, extending his right hand with the money belt.

Jeff moved toward him and reached out with both hands to make the exchanges.

"I'll meet you here when I come back from Louisville," Cry said.

Chapter 5

On the train moving toward
Louisville, Cry did not read. The fact that
his father had come in person with the
rifles and ammunition from New Jersey
and Troy, New York, Pap's hometown
when the war began, caused him to be
uneasy.

*If only I had taken the train from
Nashville* he thought *Forrest would be
grazing with mares, siring colts.*

He had often wondered what he
would have done with Alyx if his uncle,
cousin, and the teamsters had not been at
the depot that day so long ago, a day for
him that had not yet become a distant
memory. Perhaps he would have freed her
in Louisville or...

His father had come to Kentucky to
take him home a few weeks after he began
to work for Pap and had spend most of a
week in Madison County, visiting Cassius
Clay, searching for Forrest, but being
cautious, for it was Clay who told him *no
man who owns slaves in the area can be
trusted except me and my abolitionist
friends fault me for keeping my slaves so
long even though I've bought their family
members and set them free, too. They don't
like me keeping my house staff and a few
families here at Whitehall.* Clay also said
*the young man who shot your son, being as
he admittedly rode with the mob that drove*

Fee's villagers from Berea, will not be betrayed. And it turned out that no one had been found in Richmond or Mt. Vernon, with any knowledge of any shooting or horse theft near Berea.

His father had not said anything to him about the horse in the year that he was laid up. At times, he even seemed to be the troubled one. Cry had tried to tell him how sorry he was that he had failed to bring the horse to New York. He had tried to tell his father about the woman, Alyx, and why he had taken the steamboat instead of the train, but his father made frequent trips, business or otherwise during those days and nights and never appeared to have time to hear any of it. Cry had decided the trips were his father's way of dealing with the disappointment he must have felt with his only son. His father, having returned from one of his journeys in the minutes before dawn, was in bed on the morning that he left for Kentucky and Camp Dick Robinson.

Jeff had been Cry's only contact with his father and only a few words had been passed back and forth between them. Before coming to Kentucky himself, his father had sent Jeff to check on him when he had only been at Camp Dick Robinson for a week.

He wants to know what he can do? Jeff had said.

Help the General arm his volunteers he had said, handing his cousin the first knapsack of money to take North.

Cry wished he had kept a log, a journal of each time he and Jeff met thereafter. There would have been a list of names, including Lottie Moon in Oxford, Ohio who had left General Ambrose Burnside standing at the altar to marry Jim Clark, a pro-Southern politician. Lottie and her sister, Ginnie, in Memphis, ran messages for the Confederates. He had intercepted a message from Ginnie to Forrest when he introduced himself to her as a cotton buyer for an English firm. They had talked about Forrest briefly, but when she asked him if he would be seeing Forrest, he had told her he had hopes of meeting him within a week.

How is it that you know Forrest? she had asked.

When he was a slave trader, I did business with Bedford...

At the mention of his name, the one his friends used, Ginnie had asked him to deliver a letter which he promised he would. It was the letter that had disclosed the name of the gunsmith Jeff would meet...

Of all the information that he had gathered, one story had upset him. Walker Taylor, one of the best Confederate secret service men, a man he could recognize by sight, had told Lottie a story and she had passed it along to Ginnie. Cry had wanted to ask Walker if what Ginnie had told him was true—that he, having escaped capture at Fort Donelson, had planned to kidnap Lincoln and deliver him to Jefferson Davis. Cry had never had an opportunity to talk with Walker about Ginnie's tale. They had met once in Louisville, traveling in opposite directions by train and, no doubt, using false identities. They had tipped their hat at each other, but exchanged no other greetings.

He had decided, *wisely* he said to himself, not to keep notes or confide in others, for the things he did carried a heavy penalty. If he were caught gathering intelligence or running arms, he would face death by hanging or death by a firing squad. Recording such activities would make covert things best left in obscurity real—the kind of tangible evidence that could be used against him.

Disembarking at the Louisville depot, Cry saw his father at once. Even as he got close enough to see his father's face, he knew the man was not looking at him. As he walked nearer, so close that he could see his father's eyes, he thought *I have never looked on a face so marked with sadness.*

"What's wrong, father," he asked.

A smile came across the man's lips as he looked up and recognized his son. They hugged briefly, then his father stepped back.

"We've got to get the gun stacks on the train. You've got to go back at once."

"I was planning on it," Cry said. "What's wrong?"

"Grant means to come to Nashville and take command of Thomas' army like he did when you were in Chattanooga. Your general has to attack at once or he'll be reassigned to some remote outpost like Pope was and never be seen or heard from by the public again."

"How is Lincoln?"

"He supports your man now. The word in Washington is good where Lincoln is concerned. A Cipher Clerk for the War Department told me he kept a message that Lincoln never sent. It was meant for a critic of General Thomas. I wrote down what he said. Here it is. Listen to this: *It is doubtful whether his heroism and skill, exhibited last Sunday, has ever been surpassed in the world.*

"It's about time," Cry said.

"I got to see the three Booth brothers in *Julius Caesar* a couple of weeks ago. John played Marc Anthony, Edwin played Brutus, and Junius played Cassius. I wish you could have been home. It was a standing room only crowd. I know you've wanted to see Edwin. To my way of thinking, he's better than his brothers. I only got to see their father, Junius, on stage once. When you were too young to go with us, your mother and I..."

Cry realized that his father was being too chatty.

"The soldiers can load the crates," Cry said. "Tell me what's going on with you..."

"The Clay stallion was sold to a young man in Lexington who rode with Morgan," his father began...

"Forrest," Cry said...

"That's right," his father said. "If the soldier is still alive, he'll be with Forrest tomorrow and with any luck, so will the horse."

Cry felt a heaviness leave his body with those words.

"What about the one who shot me?"

"Best I could find out, he died at Vicksburg..."

Alyx, Cry thought *what happened to you?*

"I'm sorry," his father said.

"Don't be," Cry said. "It's got to the place where it wouldn't have made any difference if I killed him had we met face to face. At first, that was all I wanted... *The same way Alyx had felt about her grandfather* he thought..."

"I'm glad you didn't run into him, son. What I'm really sorry about is the girl..."

Cry could not believe what he had heard his father say...

"The girl?"

"The slave girl," he said. "The one you came out of Nashville with..."

Cry just knew that the next words his father spoke would tell him that Alyx was dead. A greater heaviness swelled up inside him...

Chapter 6

As he rode the train toward Nashville, Cry did not immediately read the *Harper's Weekly* newspapers that Jeff had given him at Franklin. What his father had told him at the 9th and Broadway passenger station in Louisville first made him angry, but that emotion gave way to disappointment, and, the worst thing about his father's revelation was how stupid it made him feel at the moment.

Cultures create rites of passage to mark the transitions his father had begun speaking *from one stage of life to the next. When your mother was born, she was baptized. Me... I haven't taken that step yet, nor have you as far as I know. When your mother began to bleed, she was no longer a girl. I have never told your mother that I became a man when I slept with a woman older than I was.*

His father had stopped talking to look into his eyes. Cry did not speak, for he was convinced that death, the final transition, was what his father would be getting to...

My father took me to the woman under the pretext that I would be working for her and I never asked him what job the woman had for me. He left me, without one word, and did not return until the next morning. He smiled at me when I came out to meet him, but we never mentioned that woman again.

His father had stopped speaking again to look into his eyes. At the moment their eyes met, Cry knew: *Alyx was meant to be my initiation, my first sexual encounter.* Disappointment overtook him... It was not what his father had done so much that he regretted, but the knowledge that when he went to Nashville, nothing was as it had appeared to be and he had not realized it. He had never been in danger of failing. His only failure had come by his own design.

The slave girl was to be to you what the woman was to me his father had confirmed what Cry had deduced. *I have read that some African tribe sends a boy out with a spear to kill a lion in order to become a man. My father took me into the jungle of the city where no weapon was necessary. I sent you to Nashville to buy the horse and have sex with a girl...*

I have to go... was all Cry said.

Yes, you must. So much depends upon your general... You cannot hate me anymore than I hate myself for what I have done to two people... Society is rife with initiation stories—tales of the journey of the hero, son. Know this: I never wanted for you to forsake comfort, security, home to charge off into the darkness of this war where evil is master.

I have no time for hate or anger. Give my love to mother Cry had said. *But there's one thing I'd like to know. Was Old Deck part of it?*

He was and...

Forrest, too, Cry had interrupted his father.

No, not Forrest his father had answered. *Mr. Porter was not in on it until the day you bought the Fancy Gal. Deck knew he was my friend ...*

That's what he meant to tell me when he started his conversation at the Fancy Gal sale with: I know... then talked about a John Deere plow instead and that's why he had on a tailored, New York suit, one like you wore before the war... Cry had said.

I bought it for him his father had admitted. *When he would come to see me, we always went to Broadway to take in a show. I never once looked on what he was doing as depriving men, women, and children of freedom or rights. You have shown me that keeping people in slavery forces them to live always in an inward state of war. This outward war will show others that, too. Old Deck died on July fourth in '63. Fate must have played a part in it, and it was, somehow, fitting. Things happen for a reason. You've heard me say that a million times. In '26, Thomas Jefferson, who wrote the Declaration of Independence, died on the fourth of July, and a few hours before that Madison died. But for the life of me, I can't think of any reason why fate had to target you and the slave girl.*

Chapter 7

Jeff was at the depot in Franklin when the train arrived. Cry had told the engineer how important it was for the train to reach Nashville and the man had told him they would not tarry long.

" I see you got there first," Cry said as he picked up one end of a wooden gun box.

"Not by more than a minute or so," Jeff said, helping Cry load the heavy crate. "How did you know Forrest would be there? Don't answer that..."

"Any trouble?"

"No," Jeff said. "The gun's were in the cellar. I went through the pantry beneath the stairs and down...

Just like Alyx had to do when she went back home, Cry thought, not hearing some of what Jeff said.

"Forrest cussed and threatened for a half-hour after he got there, maybe more, but he finally believed the gunsmith when the man cussed the damned Yankees for raiding his house and taking his repeaters without paying for them."

"Do you know whether he means to stop this train?"

"I only heard what I told you. Did you meet Uncle Martin?"

"Yes..."

Jeff looked at him and waited for Cry to speak.

"Let's get that other crate," Cry said. "Take him what's left of the money..."

"Your father?"

"Yes," Cry said, closing the boxcar door.

"Well?"

"Well, what?"

"What did he say?"

"He said he was sorry for something—good intentions that went bad..."

"Was it about the horse?"

"Yes...Partly..."

"You want me to go with you?"

"No, Jeff. Take him the money. Tell him to keep it until he hears from me. Tell him I love him. I should have, for he has done so much more good than he will ever know. Tell him in dreams we live a thousand lives..."

"What's that supposed to mean?"

"I don't know," Cry said. "It just popped into my head."

Chapter 8

Cry picked up four pages of the February 8, 1862 *Harper's Weekly,* one of several pages that Jeff had given him. The first page was a topographical map of Kentucky, showing Mill Springs.

His eyes went to the site of that battle, for he did not need to search the entire state south to north, east to west. It was as though he were there.

He opened his eyes and read the bold print: **The point where the Rebel Genl. Zollicoffer was defeated.**

Defeated he thought. *He was killed. His army was defeated. I saw him in the wagon after he was brought to Pap's tent and laid out. He was peaceful looking in death, so unlike the hundreds of other dead and wounded of both armies.*

Zollicoffer was cared for, under the General's orders with respect—the first time Cry had seen the commander exhibit tenderness. The General had the enemy's body delivered to Louisville, then returned to Tennessee under a captured flag.

Thinking about Zollicoffer, Cry also remembered a young Lieutenant who stood calmly alone at the fence, shooting a Union officer through the body, then in foolish defiance, inviting the whole onrushing army to take him. His body, too, was sent home to Tennessee. The General had recognized him as the son of a Union sympathizer.

Jeff had told him when they met in Cincinnati later that the North began to cheer and fire cannon when they heard the news of the first substantial Union victory of the war.

It was the thing that brought the people out of their dejection following Bull Run Jeff had said, unable to conceal his excitement.

But for the General Cry had protested *the War Department recommended no award, no thanks to the commanding officer while they extended the same to men serving under him.*

What about Lincoln?

Nothing... Congressman Maynard alone sent a letter. He wrote to the General: You have undoubtedly fought the great battle of the war...

He blinked then turned to page 88, expecting to read an account of the battle. Instead, he found a two-page spread, an artist's rendition of that January 19 battlefield. It was a scene of Union soldiers, charging along a line as far as his eyes could see. In the distance there was a mountain rising up, void of timber. Most of the scene was that of a bayonet charge into the Rebel line, concentrated in the trees.

The artist was talented, but the scene was not the one he remembered.

The way it was came back to him quickly: *On Christmas, the rain was freezing and turning into snow. At the end of December, in terrible weather, Pap had begun his march in mud knee deep and his men moved so slowly in it that it was as though they were pulling plows to get the wagons and cannons through. The rains fell on nine of the first seventeen days of January and a thunderstorm dropped an inch and a half of rain during the night of the eighteenth. The ground melted beneath a man's feet. It was a warm January, more like April with the temperature in the low sixties. At six in the morning, under a heavy rain, and in pitch blackness, with a muzzle flash the battle of Mill Springs began. Zollicoffer's men came up from Beech Grove on Sunday morning, confronting Wolford's scouts first...Pap had put several lines of pickets in place to spoil any Confederate surprise.*

Cry shook his head, knowing that many Union lives could have been saved at Shiloh if pickets had been thrown out to do the same...if Grant had not been absent, protected from enemy fire, when his army was hit unaware...

And then, there they stood, the rain pouring down on them, two regiments literally feet away from each other, clubbing and bayoneting, few could get their guns to work in the heavy rainfall. On one side of the little wooden fence stood a veteran confederate regiment, its tattered battle flag waving above the men's heads.

On the other side stood a Yankee regiment, new to war, as was he, and so unaware of the horrors of it. There they stood, dealing out death while Pap's artillery swept the open field.

More Rebels he closed his eyes, watching them as they *moved up and fixed bayonets to join the line near the wooden fence. Many men in place there threw away their useless muskets and pulled out foot long bowie knives that glinted in the rain. They started a charge.*

Fighting behind and in front of the fence was fierce, decimating as soldiers who could fire their guns did so at men only a few feet away. At the fence, the Rebels had held out valiantly until they were forced to withdraw from a flanking fire by the Yankees from the Ohio Ninth. Cry learned some hours later that Colonel Kise had ordered the first Union bayonet charge, led by Ohio and Minnesota infantries.

He remembered seeing another Rebel charge, led by a man, his long red hair a flag in the wind, routing the Ohio soldiers to take the fence once more. It was later in the battle that General Thomas, ever present, prepared, sharing the danger with his men, ordered a bayonet charge and the Rebels left the field, disorganized and panic stricken. That was how he remembered the battle, for he was near that wooden fence.

He studied the picture again, wishing he could draw with such skill and remembering, as he always did when he wished to be an artist, Alyx. Sometimes he felt guilt when he remembered her. At other times he felt pain. At the moment all he felt was shame. He had not gotten over being angry with himself for the way things played out when his father told him what was to have been. In the next moment, however, he felt warmth, the old attraction that does not depend upon desire alone...

He scanned the first page of four new pages, yellow from exposure to prolonged dampness in Jeff's knapsack. He read an article about Major-General John Pope. The story, dated July 12, 1862, was written at a time when the officer was still in favor with Washington, still one of Lincoln's men.

The writer opened with a statement about Pope being appointed to the command of the Army of Virginia then gave a brief history of the man's career. He had been chosen to escort President Lincoln to Washington. There was mention of his *brilliant dash* that took New Madrid by storm and an emphasis on his having arrived in Washington to receive his appointment, with Fremont, Banks, and McDowell under him...

He thought about his father's reference to Pope in his warning about General Grant's plan...

He felt uneasy about Forrest and his cavalry... If Forrest chose to do so, he could have his men derail the train and problems for Pap would be serious if not disastrous...

His thoughts returned to the Battle of Mill Springs. At that wooden fence, he had realized that the everyday soldier, Southern or Northern, had no clear idea why he was fighting. There was a wounded Rebel soldier, left behind with others when the Noble Ellis was burned on the south side of the Cumberland River.

"*What's your name, soldier,*" he had asked when he came upon him, propped against a large, shell shattered oak.

"*Ganaway Grider,*" he had answered without hesitation. "*You?*"

"*Martin Kreider,*" Cry could hear his voice, as clear as though he had only just spoken the words.

"*Cuzens...*"

"*What did you say?*" Cry had asked.

"*We kinfolks. Martin Krider come to Pennsylvania from the old country with two brothers. We jest clum down differin lems...*"

The man's words made him pause and think. He had heard similar stories, but the common thread was always that there were three brothers...

"*What can I do for you?*" he had asked.

"Take me down river," had been his request. *My sister, my uncles, my grandfather live near Creelsboro."*

He took the man back to the river to a spot where he had discovered a small boat when he had come scouting toward Beech Grove ahead of the soldiers. What he had found was that every able bodied man had gone, the camp cluttered with supplies, cannon, and mules had been abandoned. The mules were a prize. Of all things military that had been abandoned, the mules had made General Thomas smile. Cry had put the man in the boat and shoved it into the swift, muddy water...

He picked up the November 22, 1862 *Harper's Weekly,* only four pages of the original that began with an article about General McClellan, commander of the Army of the Potomac who had been called the boy Napoleon for his early victory at Rich Mountain. The glory and proclamations of victory won with a display of Napoleonic flourish faded when Lincoln decided the general had *the slows.*

Now it was Grant and the Washington politicians, seeking to remove Pap.

Calling him slow as they are means nothing less Cry thought.

Cry soon realized that Forrest would not attack them. The train would reach Nashville safely. He breathed deeply, relieved and turned the page to find a two-page illustration of the army of the Ohio on the march. The scenes, depicting General Smith's arrival at Camp Wild Cat and seven other events, he recognized at once. Studying the illustration, he shook his head. *More likely than not, I am the man on the grey horse in the drawing entitled **Distributing the Mails**.*

The grey would have been the horse the General traded him for his new wagon. The artist had captured the demeanor of the horse, not that of a race horse, but of a work animal. The horse the General had called Rebel would not flinch at the sound of rifle, pistol, nor cannon fire. The one incorrect detail in the illustration, however, was the fact that the rendition of Rebel was one of a horse with two pointed ears. In reality, during cavalry training or in a skirmish before Cry got him, a saber had amputated the tip of its right ear. When he was discovered while spying on Joe Johnston's camp at Dalton, Cry had ridden Rebel hard crossing an open field toward the cover of dense trees. Cry knew the moment Rebel took a lead ball. Rebel did not neigh or scream a horse's cry of pain, but he stumbled, faltering only once, only to die on the move when the pickets had abandoned the chase.

He smiled as he viewed the part of the print entitled: *The first snow of the season,* for it fell when the leaves were yet green, breaking the timber with cracking echoes like cannon fire at a distance. He did not smile at the portion of the illustration labeled: *Rush to the haystack* for the picture would say more to the soldiers who were there without blankets—who slept outside on the ground while killing frost covered the land—valley to mountaintops—than it would to the average reader.

Reading was the only thing that could take Cry's mind off his father, Alyx, Old Deck, and Bedford Forrest. He picked up the last of the pages that Jeff had given him, the October 10, 1863 *Harper's Weekly*. On page 641 there was a portrait of General George H. Thomas, taken by Brady, with the caption: *the hero of the Battle of Chickamauga, or Chattanooga.*

Pap was not one to talk about himself. Besides telling him about teaching the slaves to read the only other personal information that Cry knew with any certainty was the fact that his family had disowned him for choosing to fight for the Union. For his family, the General died the day he made his decision to stand with the North. His sister had written him as much, saying it would be best if he changed his name.

From the article Cry found out that Pap was born in Southampton County, Virginia, in July 1816. Cry also learned many other facts. The General was appointed to West Point in 1836 and graduated on July 1, 1840, with an appointed to the Third Artillery. *In 1841,*

Cry read, *he distinguished himself in the war against the Florida Indians, and was brevetted First Lieutenant for his gallantry.*

I have never met a braver man Cry thought *not in this war...*

As he read, he remembered the soldiers talking about Buena Vista, where, according to the news writer, he distinguished himself nobly, and was brevetted Major.

It was at Murfreesboro Cry remembered being told although he could not remember the soldier who said it: *Pap took fire from the whole Mexican Army from six in the morning until late in the afternoon. They never overran his artillery.*

It was at Murfreesboro, during a Council of War, so the General told him , that he woke up and said the Army could not run away from a field of battle; said it was as good a place to die as any he could think of...

Cry learned from the article that the General was an Instructor of Artillery and Cavalry at West Point in 1850, and in May, 1861, he was appointed Colonel of the Cavalry after the Colonel, Robert E. Lee, and the Lieutenant-Colonel, joined the Confederacy.

He knew, having been at Camp Dick Robinson himself, that Pap, in August of 1861 had received the appointment of Brigadier-General of Volunteers, and proceeded to Kentucky, dubbed the West.

It was he who, when all around seemed black and hopeless, restored joy to the hearts of loyal people by the victory of Mill Springs Cry read, recalling Jeff's words exactly. Scanning again, he read the part about Buell, the President's appointment of Pap and Pap's refusal to accept the post, the appointment of General Rosecrans, and the General's corps in the Army of the Cumberland.

He read every word of the article without pause: *At the recent Battle of Chickamauga his skill, and the unfaltering courage of his troops, saved us from an irreparable disaster, and he is justly entitled to be considered the hero of those bloody days.*

Whenever I charged their flank they broke, said General Thomas, Cry read, his heart pounding like it had on that Saturday little more than a year ago. *The charge of Longstreet's corps should go down to posterity in language that would insure the immortality of the story. Moving with admirable precision, yet with great rapidity...*

He wished he could read those words to Grant and Sherman...He knew that Grant would have seen them, but he doubted Sherman had, unless he had learned of them through correspondence with Grant.

He closed his eyes and the field lay before him, as clear as though he were stepping back on it. Men and horses littered the clearing. *Civilians have no idea what a battlefield looks like* he thought. It would be impossible for any reader other than a soldier to envision a field covered with bodies, dead and wounded so closely stacked that a man could walk across them without his feet touching the ground. The pounding in his chest intensified as he remembered how it had been to stand there when Longstreet exploited an opening that routed the Union right and center, leaving the rest of them to face death alone. They fought on that first day.

On Sunday, it had been, he recalled: *twenty-five charges by Longstreet, plus ten or twelve by Forrest and his men, dismounted, fighting like infantry. There was the moment when the fear of dying left me as the entire Rebel line came on, one after the other. The General held, refusing to break as McCook and Crittenden had done.*

He remembered how inadequate the ammunition he brought back and distributed to the men had been. He could see General Thomas sitting on his horse in the hollow of a ridge in the open field, watching a heavy cloud of dust in his rear while the ammo was being passed around.

Despair had set in when he returned, for everyone knew one more charge could not be repulsed. If the dust was the enemy, it would have to be cavalry. There was no way to repulse another fight in front much less repulse an enemy both front and rear. The ammunition would have been used up in four or five volleys. Bayonets would not have been able to save them. There would have been no escape, no surrender...

It cast a cloud over his spirits which was plainly visible to one who observed him, as I confess the writer had written of Pap *I did that day, with ever-increasing admiration.*

He read the article, the pounding in his chest, the throbbing behind his eyes subsiding. Every event that the reporter described was equally clear: the General too shaken to use his field glass, Captain Johnston reporting to Pap for duty when he was cut off from General Negley, risking his life to find out for Pap whose force was approaching.

The reporter wrote: *in a few minutes he again emerged from this timber, and following him came the red, white, and blue crescent-shaped battle-flag of Gordon Granger.*

Just before the last charge began, seven generals had gathered. Cry silently called their names: *Thomas, Granger, Garfield, Steedman, Whittaker, Wood, Grannan*, as well as *Colonel Harker.*

When the charge began, the commanders returned to their troops, except for Garfield who was dispatching HQ and Thomas, on his horse, and Granger. The reporter described an omen that Cry had missed, for he was fighting, renewed like everyone around him. He wrote of Pap: *His eyes glanced from right to left as the shell and canister exploded about the field, and once I saw him, just as the fight opened, most furiously glance up at a large, beautiful white pigeon or dove which alighted upon a dead tree above him and watched the battle from her dangerous nest.*

Having finished the article, Cry could not put the newspaper aside. He reread bits and pieces of other articles about the battle at Chickamauga, beginning with: *some ten thousand men in killed, wounded, and missing; and a number of guns...*

One article dealt with Rosecrans, the commander at Chattanooga: *At latest accounts Rosecrans was undisturbedly fortifying himself at Chattanooga, and there were no indications of an immediate resumption of the fight. It stands to reason, however, that the struggle will be renewed at a very early day. If the rebels cannot retake Chattanooga the Confederacy is gone.*

There was no account of what actually happened at Chattanooga. Some writers he had read had fallen under the impression that it was the unique battle of the war, planned from beginning to end and fought as planned, and that Grant's own army of the Tennessee played the dominant role that led the way to victory.

Cry had frowned as he read those words before, but he did not frown now, for he knew the truth. He could not keep from being angry now as he rode toward Nashville. The only way to promote such a theory was to downgrade the General to upgrade Grant and Sherman. The reporters had done it subtly at first.

Cry understood that the General had initiated and implemented changes in Grant's battle plans, but he was not the only one, for many understood why it was necessary for the changes to be made.

Cry had seen Pap's strategy develop when he took Orchard Knob instead of demonstrating toward the rifle pits as Grant had ordered. Cry could see at the time that the move shortened the distance to Missionary Ridge and more importantly opened the left flank, which allowed direct communication with Sherman. Cry was present when the General argued with Grant to let Hooker use some of Sherman's stranded men, which he finally did after it became apparent that Sherman would not break free. Hooker then cleared the right flank

Cry, more than ever, admired how Pap was aware of Hooker's progress. The semaphore messaging system he had used before Hooker's march, indeed, worked well.

The General had gotten his men where he needed them to be so they could move freely to either flank to supply reinforcements or supplies or move to support Sherman as ordered by Grant. He had already removed the barrier on his left flank of having to cross the Tennessee River twice to get to Sherman. Sherman, not being able to break out, had tied up a division and a couple of Cleburne's brigades on Bragg's right.

Cry could not help smiling when he remembered how the General got into the position he needed to be in to reduce casualties and also succeeded in getting Grant to understand. He had done it in a way that made Grant think the triumph and glory would eventually be Sherman's.

Pap, not caring who did it, but that it *got done,* Cry recalled what he had believed since that day: *Pap had presented Grant an overwhelming victory, in a style not seen on any other battlefield.* After Sherman's attack failed, when it was getting late, Grant finally gave in. When the Army of the Cumberland provided a victory using Pap's plan, Grant, disgruntled, began to ask who had given the order to take the ridge...

Chapter 9

When Cry got off the train at Nashville, he went directly to General Thomas who stood on the platform surveying the train left to right.

"How was your trip?" the General called out as soon as he spotted Cry.

"Productive, sir," Cry answered. "I know you've not been idle..."

"Far from it...Both armies have been ice-bound for a week now, but the weather has moderated. I'm prepared to move. I've called a meeting of the corps commanders for this afternoon to discuss the plan of attack so it will be thoroughly understood..."

"At least Grant's not here calling the shots, confusing things like he did at Chattanooga," Cry said.

"I'm going to lay out all the messages from Grant so my men can read them," the General said.

Cry decided not to tell him that Grant was on his way to Washington to get permission to take over the operation himself.

"I want you to be there, Cry. Get there before we do. I've left orders at the front desk for you to pick up the key to the room adjoining mine. Open the door between us so you can listen, but keep the room dark. I'm going to ask Wilson to stay behind after the meeting. At the last Council of War, he was adamant that I should wait for this thaw so he could get his cavalry refitted and ready to move."

Cry went to the St. Cloud Hotel, Pap's headquarters, and let himself into the adjoining room. While he waited for the General and his commanders to arrive, he sat in a chair with his feet propped up. It was not long before he nodded off for a while.

Cry?

He opened his eyes.

"Alyx?" he asked.

Awake, he closed his eyes in order to see. At Louisville, he had heard her voice while he and his father took leave of each other. He had looked up, he remembered and there was only his father walking away, and a man rushing toward the train...

How man times have I heard your voice, Alyx? There was the night in Chattanooga before Grant arrived he began to answer his own question. He had gone to the brothel his pockets full of gold, Federal gold the General had given him with no questions asked. Pap had never asked him who his informants were or how much money it cost to get information from them. Cry had, however, told him about needing the gold to take to the brothel...

Joe Hooker had told them during their first meeting in Chattanooga, intelligence gathering being the topic of discussion, that when McClellan left the Army of the Potomac, he took Allan Pinkerton, and all his agents, as well as all the secret files with him, leaving behind John Babcock, the only enlisted man working in the intelligence gathering network. McClellan's replacement, Ambrose Burnside did not rebuild the intelligence bureau. However, one of the first things Hooker did when he replaced Burnside was to organize his own information command under Colonel Joseph Sharpe.

What sources have you used? Hooker had asked the General.

Pap had given him a list that included soldier spies who ran the risk of being hanged if caught, intercepted cavalry personal and field reports, paid informants, runaway slaves, prisoners, deserters and a Signal Corps.

Have you used balloonists? Hooker had asked.

Never had one Pap had answered. *You ever used a brothel?*

Never had one Hooker had laughed. *What have you learned from the ladies?*

Cry the General had said. *Tell him what the ladies told you...*

Bragg's men have lost all faith in him. What is worse, his commanders have lost faith in him as well. No one wants to obey him, follow him, or fight for him, but they will. I don't think they'll stick long.

Forrest cussed him—threatened him— walked out on him after Chickamauga, Cry had said.

Do your men use the same brothel?

Do they? the General had asked, turning to Cry.

They do, sir...

First thing you need to stop Hooker had warned. *I learned the hard way that when my Pickets talked with enemy pickets, traded newspapers, and cigarettes at flag of truce meetings, the Rebels learned what moves I was planning. I like to think my intelligence service is at least as good as General Lee's now...*

I would say my intelligence service is at least as good as yours Pap had answered.

Then how can we best utilize them? Hooker had asked.

Our Signal Corps officers need to meet and learn to speak the same language had been the General's answer.

At the brothel when he thought he heard Alyx's voice call out: *Cry,* he had turned quickly, facing a young woman who stood in the doorway of her room, but through a crack in the doorway he had seen a Billy Blue uniform.

You from Kentucky? he had asked.

How'd you know?

You sounded like a woman I once knew...

Stick around, Cry, she had said *and you can get to know me all you want...*

I don't think our mutual friend behind the door would want me to do that...

He won't mind. He's the one told me your name she had said...

Git in here, woman! the man behind the door had yelled.

Cry got up. Putting the scene out of mind, he walked around the room to regain the feeling in his right leg. He returned to the chair and sat down, thinking *I can't begin to count the times I've heard you call my name...*

Chapter 10

Cry sat in the chair, fighting sleep, nodding until he remembered the night he had dreamed he was making love to Alyx, the time she had pricked him with her dagger. He knew that the dagger was not what had kept him from trying...

The dream he thought. Although he was unable to recall all of it, he remembered: *giving a stallion to his father... and Alyx was with him... and the steamship with food...*

Do you believe, Cry, that dreams come from the future? The General's words, spoken in the next room a few day before he went to Louisville, came back to him.

Perhaps the steamship in the dream, loaded with food, and the starving men unloading, was really the steamboat Pap's engineer's built down river from Chattanooga after the wagon train of supplies was destroyed. Perhaps the boat was the sternwheeler that brought sacks of food up the shallow rapids to put an end to Bragg's plan of starving the Union forces into surrendering the city.

If there are things that are meant to outlast all of us he told himself *war has to be one of them. War is not* he nodded *a gift that keeps a man...* he slept—woke—had kept the thought, finishing it: *or a woman human.*

He slept. He dreamed: *by the clear river, a cedar, straight, tall, without a limb at all for twenty or thirty feet, surrounded by budding poplars almost as tall as the cedar is tall, falls for no reason, falls silently. He sits beneath the tree until he feels the pressure of the trees pushing down on him. He jumps up and runs...*

In the next room, voices put an end to his dream...

He listened...

Chapter 11

Cry listened to the General and his commanders talk. As he had said he would, the General must have spread out the messages from Grant.

"I want all of you to read these. If you have anything to say, let's get it out now.

Cry heard every commander speak except for Schofield.

Pap explained his orders for battle and no one spoke out against the plan.

"Be ready to move out early in the morning," Pap said as the meeting came to an end.

Cry heard the commanders leaving one by one and heard the General speak: "If you don't mind to stay behind, I'd like to speak with you."

Cry recognized Wilson's voice, "Be glad to, sir..."

"They treat me as if I were a boy," the General said. "They seem to think me incapable of planning a campaign or of fighting a battle. If they will just let me alone... I will show them what we can do."

"My men are ready, sir. The weather was a blessing. No one would have thought just a week ago that my men would be remounted... Is that Cry in the next room?"

"It is," the General said. "Come on in..."

Cry walked out of the darkness into the light, stopping a few feet from the two men.

"We have about fifteen thousand magazine fed Spencer rifles, son. I want to thank you."

"No need, sir..."

"You've been around this man so long," Wilson pointed at General Thomas, "that you talk like him..."

"I take that as a compliment," Cry said.

"As it was meant," Wilson said. "I wouldn't worry about Washington, General, if I were you. After..."

There was a knock on the door. Cry went back into the dark, adjoining room and sat down in the chair.

"Come in, sir," Wilson said. "I'm leaving General. My men and I will not be late in the morning. You two should sleep better tonight."

"Hopefully," Cry recognized the voice at once as Steedman's...

"Is there a problem, my friend?"

"I've been doing some detective work ever since General Whipple told me someone was sending telegrams to Washington to undermine you, sir!"

"He told me the same thing, but I haven't had a chance to look into it yet. Have you learned something?"

"Captain Davis picked up this message from the trash after it was sent, sir..."

"Many officers here," Pap read aloud," are of the opinion that General Thomas is certainly too slow in his movements..."

"I want you to know that those words..."

"Could it be possible?" the General asked, his tone subdued.

"As I was about to say, sir," Steedman said, "there can only be one officer here who would send that lie."

"And who might that be?"

"You should be familiar with the handwriting of your own General, sir..."

"Let me put on my glasses," the General said. "Yes it is..."

"The one who is next in command of you?"

"Oh, I see," the General said. "Thank you..."

"What does a man need for thanks," Steedman laughed.

Cry smiled.

"We shall all be ready by 5:00 AM, even the one," Steedman said, taking his leave.

Cry came into the room as soon as he heard the door close.

"What do you make of that?" Pap asked.

"I will make certain that my bead is on the man who did not speak tonight..."

"No need for that, son. I will keep a tight rein on him tomorrow. Go rest... You must be tired..."

"I need some gold," Cry said. "Hood's spies will be out in force tonight in this city."

"Use what you need," Pap said, taking a money belt from beneath the pillow on his bed. "Sir Walter Scott was the premier poet for the South before this war began. War destroys culture, don't you think, Cry?"

"War is no respecter of anything a man holds dear, sir..."

"Thomas Moore, the Irish poet was the people's favorite in Richmond, I know. My sisters loved his words. I doubt they find time for reading these days."

"Greece, everything Greek, poetry, painting, architecture, took New York by storm," Cry said.

"Lord Byron with his cult of Greece and his romantic notions," Pap said, "I think you read him, don't you?"

"I've seen you buy those books, sir," Cry said.

"For my wife," the General laughed. "You do read him?"

"His words work on me like they are my own thoughts," Cry said.

"So it was with *The Lady of the Lake.* That book took the South by storm. Southerners thought of themselves as proud knights ready to do or die for some romantic ideal. This land is no longer a place of fine lords and fair ladies."

"It never will be again, sir..."

"I fear you are right. Where men once delighted to meet women in the field of letters and in the arena of social life, chivalry and romance appear to be dying around us. I wonder which knights will survive this rebellion?"

"Sir Carlton and Sir Malcolm..."

"I don't believe I've ever heard of them."

"They are knights of the future, sir. Women will desire them..."

"I don't know, Cry," the General said. "I trust you know more about that than I do."

"It is not important, sir. Tonight I will mingle with your eyes and your ears. I will tell you in the morning what they have seen and what they have heard."

Chapter 12

The fog, brought on by the warming temperatures, delayed the opening of the battle. General Thomas utilized the time, however, to confer with his commanders, singly or in groups of two or three. The movement toward Pap and away from him was almost constant.

"I suppose you think I don't consider what you have learned to be of any importance, do you, Cry."

"On the contrary, sir. I know the weather is holding you up. I know the men are getting restless..."

"Hood's waiting for us," the General said.

"He's not expecting us today," Cry said.

"If only I could believe that..."

"Believe it, sir, it's true..."

"Make me happy, Cry. Tell me what we got for our money..."

"We've got men, his spies, telling him the attack will come tomorrow. He's got a woman with him who hates us. She doesn't know the truth either."

"Is she a soldier?"

"No, sir. She's a local..."

"Good. Anything else?"

"Forrest won't be here..."

"Yes!" Pap slapped his leg. "That makes me happy. When Cump set out in November on his great expedition to attack railroads and cities from Atlanta to the seaboard, he left me to guard Tennessee or to pursue Hood's unit when it came after his column."

"The days of having less than half the numbers under Hood are behind us," Cry said.

"My only resource was to gain time for reinforcements to arrive and try to concentrate..."

"You did that well..."

"It was easier to get an infantry force nearly equal to that of Hood's but not so easy getting an equal, effective cavalry. We are about to go and dispute the possession of Tennessee with Hood's army."

"Of this battle, sir," Cry said, "you must report that the position of Hood's army around Nashville remained a constant threat, and that you were busy preparing to take the offensive without delay..."

"Are you forgetting that we have not fought this battle?"

"I am only suggesting that when you have won this battle, sir, you must report that the cavalry was being remounted, under the direction of General Wilson, as rapidly as possible, and new transportation furnished where it was required..."

"You know the unit I desire most of all for this, don't you, Cry?"

"The Fourteenth, sir," Cry stated without hesitation.

"Mill Springs, Perryville, Shiloh, Corinth, Stone River, Chickamauga, Mission Ridge, Atlanta, Jonesville—Cry—the Fourteenth Army Corps was mine..."

"Wearing a crimson acorn on their chests..."

"And on their battle flags. They were an elite corps, son, the first brigade I organized at Camp Dick Robinson..."

"I remember, sir... Here..."

The General took the red acorn, wrought in gold and studded with precious stones, from Cry's hand and pinned it to his collar.

"Where..."

"I found it when we crossed the rifle pits and took Missionary Ridge, sir, about half-way up."

"Thanks, son, but I was about to ask you where yours is..."

"In my pocket for luck, Pap..."

"Sherman could not bear to see the unit with me," the General said softly. "I asked for it when he sent me here to watch for Hood. He told me: *It is too compact and reliable a corps for me to leave behind...*"

"Yet he criticized it to Grant and Halleck as..."

"How well I remember: *as entrenching at the sight of a fresh, up-*

turned furrow... My eyes and ears, as you call them, in Washington told you that..."

"You have eyes and ears where you need them, sir..."

"Tossing three potatoes in the air was one of the best moves I've made in this Rebellion..."

"I don't know if you should go so far as to say that..."

"I have said it. I like to give laurels to a man when he is living rather than send roses when he dies. Why have you stayed with me, Cry?"

"I really don't know, sir. Maybe it was Old Phil's cooking that kept me."

The General laughed and said, "Crumb said: *I can spare you the Fourth Corps and about five thousand men not fit for my purpose...*"

"There's nothing wrong with your memory, Pap. Sherman was still assuming that Hood wasn't intending to invade Tennessee..."

"And before many weeks had passed he was advising me to concentrate all my troops at one point and attack the invader."

"With those 5,000 cavalry troops minus horses and all the damaged artillery from *his surplus*," Cry said." He also said: *If he'll go to the Ohio River. I'll give him rations.*"

"Grant, however, had misgivings. You told me that," the General said. "How many times have we had these conversations, Cry?"

"This will be the last time, sir."

The General looked at him, puzzled.

"Grant felt that Sherman's chief assignment was Hood," Cry chose not to clarify his answer. "His words to your friend, Cump, were: *If you see a chance of destroying Hood's Army, do it.*"

"Washington insiders tell Grant Hood can't come to the Ohio and cause them political embarrassment, do they?"

"They do, sir."

"The casualties my troops might have suffered if I had undertaken with haste such an improvised battle as they had ordered..."

"Casualties are immaterial to them, sir..."

"The politicians?"

"Yes, sir..."

"And Grant and Cump, too? Does it appear to you that casualties have been insignificant to them all through this Rebellion?"

"You know them well..."

"Go pass along the order of battle that we have discussed... Make sure they understand what they are to do, everyone of them, that they move in the order we discussed last night. It's time... Tell them, if I see a need to change something after we begin, I'll get word to them!"

As he rode away, Cry thought about Secretary Stanton's words: *If he waits for*

Wilson to get ready, Gabriel will be blowing his last horn. Halleck had relayed a similar message to Pap. Cry had no doubts that the commanders would carry out Pap's orders, even Schofield for the General meant to keep his enemy closer than his friends. Cry knew Pap would make the man who would replace him fight when the time came. Cry also knew that Wilson was ready, not only for the attack, but for the pursuit of Hood's army. No horn was blowing as he approached Maj. Gen. A. J. Smith nor when the Army of the Tennessee began its vigorous assault on the enemy's left.

Chapter 13

"I gots duh cabinets put in," Ben Singleton told Cry. Ben, who like the General was called Pap by his friends, had been a former slave, born and raised in Tennessee, who was sold, sent to New Orleans. He escaped, returned to Nashville, and went to Detroit to be free.

"Here," Cry said, extending his right hand with a small, draw string, white pouch in it.

"I thanks ya, Cry," Pap said, without opening the pouch to count the gold pieces that Cry had given him as payment for the repairs that he had done to the house Cry's aunt and uncle had abandoned.

"What made you come back to Nashville. Pap?"

"Ise can make it here," he answered, "builden cabinets and coffens. Most my peoples got nutten for skills cepten been slaves. Ise preechen ta 'em hows goen west ta farm, on day own land be what day gots ta do..."

"That's good advice, Pap. Federal homestead lands will disappear quickly though..."

"Ya gwine ta libe hyar atter day war?"

"I don't know, Pap."

"Mabbe ya otter go west, Cry. Ise gots ta go. Ise thanks ya fur duh work. Ise gots coffens ta make fur dem dead soldiers."

"Don't let me keep you, Pap. I'm just going to sit here a while and watch the boys play war."

"Ya wants me to work more jest cum down ta duh ribber..."

"When you get caught up, Pap," Cry said. "You can start on the front porch. I put some extra in for that. There should be enough lumber inside the house to make the repairs."

"I seed hit. Ya gwine atter dem debils agin?"

"I'm going out with the cavalry in the morning, Pap..."

"Ise hope ya gets up wid duh hoss and duh gal..."

"Who told you about them?"

"Duh Genrul," Pap said. "He say ya mabbe not cum bak..."

"You tell the General I'll see him again."

"Yassa, Cry. Ise shore nuf weel..."

Cry watched the man walk away toward the right—watched until he disappeared in the trees by the Cumberland river. On the hillside to his left, a group of eighteen small boys, blacks and whites, had gathered to play war. At the bottom of the hill, behind a breastwork of limbs and rubble, a group of seven older boys waited, determined to drive back the smaller warriors again.

Since the battle of Nashville, Cry had watched the boys fight the war in their own way. Before Ben arrived, three of the smaller boys had told him how a few days ago, about a dozen of them agreed to fight. After deciding the smaller boys would represent the Federals and the bigger boys the Rebels, the former took possession of the hill, and the latter went below. Each day, reinforcements had arrived to join the battle. The Union soldiers had not won a fight.

Before the larger boys had arrived for the daily battles, Cry had called out to the smaller boys and after they had gathered around him, he explained how the General had planned his battle.

"You are General Thomas," he had said to the smallest boy in the group. "Here's what you do..."

After waiting to see whether Hood would attack his Federals, the boy, Thomas, doing as Cry had suggested, ordered a charge upon the Rebel forces, using his black soldiers under a small Steedman to begin an attack on the Rebel right. After the attack began, down the hill the different divisions rushed at full speed, each armed with a stick. Cry laughed when the Johnnies dropped their sticks, as the Feds, being unable to stop their headlong charge, dashed into their Rebel lines. Before they could regroup, three of the larger, make believe soldiers were taken prisoners. The other Rebel soldiers ran headlong toward the river.

"What should we do with them, Mr. President?" the small boy General Thomas, arriving a few yards ahead of the other players, asked Cry.

"Well, General," Cry smiled, "I think you should pardon any of them who will take an oath not to fight against you again and hang the ones who won't..."

"You heard the President," the boy General said. "Who wants to take an oath not to fight against the Union again?"

Three hand went up.

"What are your plans, now, General?" Cry asked.

"Yesterday some Johnnies dug entrenchments near the Capitol, sent out scouts, reconnoitered the neighborhood, and drove us back to these lines. I think I'll march my men over there and flank their breastworks. We've got most of an hour until our mammas expect us home."

"Well, good luck to you, sir," Cry saluted.

"Thank you, Mr. President," the boy General returned the salute. "Fall in! Forward march!"

The boys began a rapid march up the hillside. Before they reached the summit, the three larger boys ran after them, holding a conference with the boy General. In a moment, the General ran back down the hill toward Cry.

"Mr. President," the boy General, gasping for breath asked, "would it be possible for the prisoners to join up with us."

"Yes, sir, General," Cry said. "It happens all the time. Just make them take an oath to support the Union and give them big sticks. Call them your cavalry. See those two boys down there coming out of the trees by the river?"

"Yes, sir, Mr. President, I do..."

"I think they're deserters. You might want to administer the same oath to them."

"I will, Mr. President, and sir..."

"What, General?"

"We're gonna win this war for you," the boy General saluted.

"I'm proud of you, sir," Cry saluted.

The boy General saluted and ran off to join his playmates.

Chapter 14

"I'm going to leave you, sir," Cry had told the General three days before he met the cabinet maker and watched the boys play their war games.

His lips knotted for a moment, Cry remembered.

"You should join up with Wilson..."

"I need to find Forrest before he does," Cry said.

"The formation I used with the troops when we went after Hood, and being partially concealed by the broken ground, as well as by that dense fog, which only lifted toward noon—that formation was important, but when you told me Hood would be totally unaware of any attack on his position—those words braced me..."

"Your strategy, the diversion to his right while your thrust would come against his left, weakened Hood, routed him both days. Your ability is, without a doubt, what is causing Grant to split your army now. In that hotel room before the battle, I wanted so much for you to send your words about his having a hundred thousand men against Lee in the East and not being able..."

"Those words were spoken in anger and desperation, son."

"In your report, did you mention that the assault was made, and received by the enemy with a tremendous fire of grape and canister and musketry?"

"I will..."

"I think Schofield will attempt to play down the battle, sir..."

"You're probably right. In my first battle report, in the Mexican War, I only wrote a few lines," the General said.

"You were not seeking fame, sir..."

"Not then or ever, Cry. I will include every command, Steedman's colored troops, Smith and Wilson's wheeling to the left and advancing against the enemy's position, Wood's ordered assault on Overton's Hill."

"I saw Colonel Morgan's men move across open ground, saw them, wounded-- black and white indiscriminately mingled-- lying amid the abatis..."

"It will be a most detailed and lengthy report, Cry. I won't skip a beat in it...Schofield had his moments."

"In that case, write that your pontoon crew, the one you trained properly, with its efficient engineers, was taken by Sherman..."

The General smiled.

"I will miss your eyes and ears, Cry."

"You have won the war here, General. Napoleon's got nothing on you, sir. You do not need me any more."

"Do you think Forrest will fold?"

"You know he won't. I went with Wilson in pursuit of Hood. You know what happened..."

The General picked up a pile of papers, shuffled through them and looked down, saying as he scanned: "With the exception of Forrest as his rear guard, Hood's army..." Then reading, he continued: "*became a disheartened and disorganized rabble of half-armed and barefooted men, who sought every opportunity to fall out by the wayside and desert their cause to put an end to their sufferings.*"

"Forrest is undaunted and firm. His men will continue to do their work bravely to the last," Cry said.

"Cump still wants Forrest dead, but he knows that it's not possible to kill him with wants... Cump knows the man's cavalry will travel a hundred miles while his own will only cover ten as they move toward the sea."

"I've got to find Forrest before Wilson does," Cry repeated. "He probably knows something about my father's horse."

"You'd best leave soon. Grant would only agree to me giving Wilson a free hand to continue the pursuit of Hood's army..."

"You can trust Wilson..."

"I know, Cry. Just before the final break through on Hood's right, I heard loud cheering crossing the battlefield? Do you know what I said?"

"No, sir..."

"I said it was the voice of the American people. Then I rode out to find Wilson and when I found him, I said *Dang it to hell, Wilson, didn't I tell you we could lick 'em, didn't I?*"

"While his cavalry passed in parade, I heard him ask you to let him defeat Forrest. I heard you tell him to make his move. He has enough Spencers to do just that."

"Go in under a flag of truce, son, for Forrest is a man of honor, but you know that..."

"Even in defeat, honor is what he lives by, sir... I sure as rain know that..."

"Cump says it will be the young men who follow Forrest and other independent commands like his that we will have to worry about when this Rebellion is over. He says they have no care—no fear at all of danger and its consequences. When I told him I knew that, I was thinking about you. What are you going to do after this Rebellion has been put down?"

"I don't know, sir. I really don't have a clue..."

Chapter 15

As Cry rode south from Nashville, the General was on his mind. *When Longstreet turned north at Chickamauga to help destroy Pap's army, Bragg was on the verge of victory. Instead, we held Snodgrass Hill...*

Forrest was also on his mind. Cry knew he would fight, lead his men to the end. Cry also knew there would be an end for Forrest, and Mississippi and Alabama as well. The end, however, would not come in a day or two, nor in a month or two. Even though Wilson, indeed all of Pap's cavalry commanders, would press Forrest, the man's will was yet strong and his personal example, his leadership abilities were much stronger than most of them who would seek him out.

Unlike the roads from Nashville, the roads through Mississippi and Alabama will not be littered with abandoned wagons, artillery, small-arms, blankets, Cry told himself *but with bodies—death will defy disorder as Forrest protects Hood's retreat.*

It was Major-General Halleck who relayed Grant's expressed order to Pap that the commander-in-chief did not intend for the army in Tennessee to go into winter quarters. Pap would issue orders tomorrow for the renewal of the campaign against the enemy in

Mississippi and Alabama, but today, tonight—until he found Forrest—Cry would travel.

Chapter 16

"And who air you, uh comin' in hyar like thiz, boy?"

"Martin Kreider, sir," Cry said.

General Forrest motioned for the sentinel to leave them alone.

"How's yore father, son?"

"He's well, sir..."

"My friends call me Bedford. My enemies, and there's shore nuf uh might of em, call me Forrest..."

"Sherman calls you that devil Forrest..."

"That sonsabitch!"

"He's afraid of you..."

"That devil Forrest... Has uh ring to hit, don't hit?"

"It does, for a fact, Bedford..."

"Who sent ya?"

"No one..."

"Noboddy?"

"Nobody," Cry said.

"The hoss is with Lyon. Mabbe still in Kentucky or mabbe on the way ta Red Hill, Alabama. Never spected ta see ya agin. I've fit all my life. Reckon ya can tell yore Pa I'd rather be plowin' with one of them John Deere and lookin' up uh mule's hind parts than be whar I am at this moment?"

"I'll tell him. The cavalry's a day or two behind me. I was sorry to hear that your brother was killed at Okolona last year..."

"Warriors dream and die, son. I thank ya...What kinda fella is this Wilson?"

"'Bout like you, Bedford, at Murfreesboro."

"Heard what I said, did ya?"

Cry shook his head.

"Then I understand he ain't comin' ta make half uh job of hit. I reckon he means ta have us all. Your General's doen what I couldn't git mine ta do after Chickamauga... We could of chased 'em and smashed 'em before thar ever was uh battle for Chattanooga. Your General knows Hood's dun us in, don't he?"

"He does, Bedford. I wish you the best..."

" I got my son with me, Martin Kreider. I wish he warn't, but history can't be dismissed. Now git! Ya got uh hard ride ahead and I got uh lot more hell ta bust wide open!"

Chapter 17

Cry came upon Colonel W. J. Palmer, commanding the Fifteenth Pennsylvania Cavalry, with one hundred fifty men, at the river crossing near Paint Rock on January fourteenth. As they rode, Palmer told Cry how Lyon was met by La Grange's brigade near Greensburg, Kentucky and after a sharp fight was thrown into confusion. Lyon had escaped by making a wide detour to Elizabethtown then to Glasgow, riding hard from there to reach the Cumberland River and cross at Burkesville...

At the mention of Burkesville, the image of Forrest, wallowing in the dust before he rode the thoroughbred for the first time, flashed before Cry's eyes...

"General Lyon proceeded from Kentucky to McMinnville then to Winchester, Tennessee. He got chased to Larkinsville, Alabama where he got on the Memphis and Charleston Railroad. He attacked the little garrison at Scottsborough. Lyon got it put to him again there and his command scattered. When he crossed the Tennessee River with one piece of artillery, his command broke into squads, taking to the mountains. We've pressed him close to Red Hill, on the road from Warrenton to Tuscaloosa, and we aim to catch him tonight."

They rode faster, not talking as darkness fell around them. When they rushed Lyon's camp later, the surprise was so complete that Lyon himself was captured along with his one piece of artillery, and almost a hundred of his men, with their horses. Even in the blackness, Forrest stood out from the other mounts. Cry took his bridle, saddle, blanket, rifle and pistols from the sorrel he had ridden and put them on the thoroughbred. The smell of the horse's sweat...

No one will understand me... Can happiness be a smell? Cry smiled for a time too short—remembered the smell of the cream that he had rubbed on Alyx and the odor of that invisible scent made him sad.

There was a shot that brought Cry back to reality. He led Forrest toward Colonel Palmer.

"What's happened?" Cry asked.

"You know how we caught Lyon in bed... You were there. Well, I wish I had used you to guard him. Man I posted over him let Lyon seize the moment and shoot him dead upon the spot. He has escaped in the darkness. Pitiful... My man has been the only casualty during this expedition.

"I'll be leaving you, sir..."

"On your way back to Nashville?"

"I am, sir..."

"Tell the General I'm off to give Hood's army another dose of medicine."

"I'll do it, Colonel. Best of luck to you..."

Chapter 18

As Cry rode, woods on either side of
him, the weather was intensely cold.
Forrest's nostrils were frosted. He did not
think about New York, but of Nashville—of
Old Deck and Alyx. He did not think about
the General's inflicting on Hood's army an
unquestionable defeat--almost an
annihilation. He thought, instead, about
the boy he had been just over six years
ago. Now a man, he told himself: *I have
found the horse, but the girl...*

The man on the platform Cry
thought: *The man rushing toward the
train... That couldn't have been Alyx...*

Journeys

Book Three

An End to Journey Towards

Chapter 1

Forrest was still fighting when Lee surrendered to Grant on April 9, 1865. He had fought almost daily since Hood's retreat from Tennessee. He had met with General Thomas' Provost Marshal, Colonel John G. Parkhurst, in February. Parkhurst had returned to Nashville with a real admiration for the Confederate general. Cry had been present during the debriefing. Parkhurst had reported that Pap's message had been delivered and Forrest had told Parkhurst that as far as guerillas were concerned, he would: *Esteem it a favor if General Thomas would hang every one caught."*

Forrest was still fighting when John Wilkes Booth assassinated Lincoln on April 14, 1865 and when Pap sent Cry to track Jefferson Davis' party as they escaped Richmond. What Forrest did in command of the rear guard of the retreating Confederate army was unexpected given the superior forces in pursuit. Pap had suggested that the acts of Marshal Ney while covering Napoleon's retreat from Moscow were the most historically similar actions ever undertaken. With only a remnant of his army hastily gathered, he made his final fight at Selma and on May 9ᵗʰ he laid down his arms. It was on that day that President Andrew Johnson issued a proclamation declaring the war's end.

It was early in the morning on the next day that the expedition in pursuit of the Confederate President's party, commanded by Lieutenant Colonel Prichard but directed by General Wilson from his headquarters in Macon, Georgia, surprised Jefferson Davis and his entourage near Abbeville, Georgia. Behind the scene, as always, was Pap. His secret service, led by Cry and other men equally aware of war, its cruelty and intimacy, were assigned to Stoneman's Division for a cavalry raid through East Tennessee, western Virginia and North Carolina. Cry and a small group of other men, never more than six, had tracked the remnants of the Confederate government from Virginia and had infiltrated the column protecting Davis at Charlotte, North Carolina. It was at Charlotte that Cry heard President Davis, during a speech, read a dispatch that was handed to him, announcing that President Lincoln had been assassinated. The Confederate president had read the dispatch aloud, making very little comment and displaying no great joy.

When General John C. Breckinridge, Secretary of the Confederate War Department, arrived in Charlotte two days after Davis, he was cheerful and hopeful that the surrender terms he had helped draft for General Johnston and General Sherman, a document approved by the President of the Confederate States, would be ratified by the Federal Government. Authorities in Washington, however, had not approved the terms, so the President of a doomed confederacy made up his mind to leave Charlotte with a select party of twenty; determined to march to Alabama where he would join up with Generals Taylor and Forrest.

On the morning of Davis' capture, Cry watched the First Wisconsin and Fourth Michigan Volunteer Cavalry fire upon each other. He shook his head in disbelief as one officer and two men of the First Wisconsin were killed.

Cry watched the President; wearing the disguise of a lady, a waterproof cloak or a robe and a shawl, lumber toward the safety of the trees where he was surrounded. He watched the President prepare to defend himself with a Bowie knife until he was convinced to surrender.

Cry had often wondered how he would feel at the end of the war, *the Rebellion as General Thomas always spoke or wrote of it.* As he searched his thoughts, he felt more relief than he did the night he found the Clay stallion alive.

Cry had waited until the dead and wounded were tied across their mounts; had waited until the President of the Confederate States of America, his family—maids and servants—his staff, his personal body guards—a colonel, a major, a captain, a lieutenant, and a midshipman of the Confederate States Navy and twelve privates—had been escorted away.

When no one else remained, Cry made his way to the place where the President had crossed the clearing and retrieved, from the space between two large boulders where Jefferson Davis had dropped it, a shot-bag before he had pulled his Bowie knife and advanced on a superior enemy force that was surrounding him. The man had drawn his enemies away from the spot like a Killdeer does when her nest or young hatchlings are approached.

Chapter 2

Cry did not begin at once to read any of the articles from the three newspapers that Jeff had sent to him. He glanced at each of the issues before he chose the *Chicago Tribune* that Chastity had brought from his cousin. He put aside two issues of *Harper's Weekly.* He had not attended Champ Ferguson's trial before an Army commission, but he had been issued one of three hundred passes to the military execution.

After he read the account, he decided he should have read the *Harper's Weekly* issue first, but he had wanted to see how the *Chicago Tribune* reported the event. He was disappointed that the newspaper had only reprinted an article from the Nashville paper.

As he read the *Harper's Weekly* article, he was disturbed by the words that painted Champ as **quite a character, though the bloodiest of rascals and murderers.** The verdict in the court martial had not been handed down when the article was written. Toward the end of the story, the reporter had written: **He surrendered at the close of the war, supposing that he would be let off with the pledge of allegiance.**

Of interest to him was the headline about Captain Henry Wirz of Andersonville Prison being found guilty and sentenced to hang. There was also an article about a petition from Italy asking that the Federal Government give mercy to Jeff Davis after his capture and immediate imprisonment at Fort Monroe.

The article that most held his attention was a reprint of the execution of Champ Ferguson, an account taken from the *Nashville Union*. The story began with the words: **Champ Ferguson is no more!**

Cry had followed the results of the trial, the verdict and the sentence in the Nashville newspaper. He skimmed the article about Champ and focused on an illustration of Champ with his eleven guards, men with bayonets affixed to rifles. Champ towered above all but three of them.

Cry closed his eyes and relived the race at Creelsboro. He regretted the fact that Forrest had been stolen and had sired no colts. He shared Champ's wish, as quoted in the *Harper's Weekly* article that: **there had never been any war**.

He turned through the pages of the November 11, 1865 edition of *Harper's Weekly* until he found the article about the execution of Champ. He read the opening words: **Champ Ferguson, the notorious guerilla, suffered the death penalty on the 20th of October.** The reporter labeled Champ **the brutal wretch...**

The illustration beneath the story, as sketched by the newspaper's artist, showed Champ, his face covered, hanging, with his body from the knees up above the trap door.

Cry had stood in the second row, looking up at Champ from the front of the scaffold. When their eyes had met, Champ had at once nodded at him and a few moments later had asked the hangman not to allow his body to be cut up by doctors, but requested that he be buried in his home soil. While Cry stood there in the crowd, the trap door dropped, Champ immediately fell from view. The front, sides, and rear of the platform, being covered with wood siding, had hidden Champ from all peering eyes, except those of the men on the platform who could have looked down.

Chastity came to the parlor where Cry sat alone.

"Would you come upstairs with me, Cry?" she asked. "There's something I'd like to ask you in private."

"I'll be right up," Cry said. "I promised Aunt Mary that I would carry in wood for the fireplace. It will be chilly tonight..."

Chapter 3

"Thanks for coming up," Chastity said, then laughing asked: "Do you suppose your aunt will have as much trouble with you being here as she did at church the first time I ever saw you?"

"She has mellowed," Cry said...

"I hate you, you know?"

"I never asked Jeff to do anything..."

"You didn't have to," she said. "He worships you—always has..."

"Let's not argue..."

"I didn't call you up here to argue," she began to sob.

"What's wrong?"

"I've cheated on Jeff," she said. "In Missouri..."

"I don't need to know this," Cry said.

"He was our neighbor. He looked so good in his uniform, and I had not seen Jeff in four months, maybe longer..."

Cry did not say anything during her silence.

She looked at him, her cheeks glistening.

"I went to bed with him. I want to know if I should tell Jeff..."

"No," Cry said. "If you don't want to marry Jeff, just tell him you can't..."

"I want to marry him—tomorrow like we've planned."

"Then do it..."

"What if he finds out?"

"How will he know?"

"We've never had sex," she said...

After a moment, Cry spoke, "Let me ask you something..."

"Sure..."

"Do you love the other man?"

"He says he loves me..."

"Says?"

"He's in Nashville..."

"A man, when he's drunk or when he thinks he might get a woman into bed, will say I love you..."

"Is that what you tell your women, Cry?"

Cry felt his face flush...

"Jeff was right!"

Cry stared at her...

"You haven't been with a woman either!"

Cry dropped his head.

"Do you know whether Jeff actually has?"

"You'll have to ask him," Cry said, looking into her eyes.

"Jeff told me about the slave girl."

"Were you raped?" Cry asked.

"No!"

"Were you drunk?"

"No! We were friends from the day my family got to Missouri."

"Was the sex great?"

"Most of the girls I've talked with say they don't even like sex. They end up doing it because they feel like it is expected of them."

"Don't tell him," Cry said. "A man doesn't have a clue...

She looked at him, puzzled.

"What about..."

"Fake it," Cry said, knowing what she meant to ask. "Whimper as though you are in pain. He wouldn't tell you, you know?"

"You don't think so?"

"Man's not expected to confess..."

"I just feel so..."

"Guilty," Cry said. "You say you still want to marry him..."

"I do."

"And the sex wasn't earth shattering, you say?"

"It was disappointing," she said.

"Marry him," Cry said. "Don't tell him... Teach him how to make love to you..."

"What?"

"A man doesn't have a clue beyond knowing how things fit together. Only a woman knows how to make love..."

"Did your slave girl tell you that?"

Only a woman knows how to make love to a woman Cry remembered Alyx's words.

"Is that how you're going to learn?" she asked.

"I should be so lucky," he answered.

Chapter 4

Chastity did not tell Jeff about her infidelity. Cry was glad she chose not to tell him about the other man. She also chose not to get married in church. Neither Jeff's parents nor Chastity's questioned why the wedding was to take place outside the city on a high point that overlooked the Cumberland River and beyond it, the Capital building at Nashville.

Cry stood beside Jeff, their backs toward the minister. He remembered the letter he had mailed to Jeff from Creelsboro. He had written that he knew Jeff would marry Chastity. He had not mentioned Alyx, but he had written that he was on a boat... That he had met a girl... As they waited, Chastity, led by her father, in her white gown still reminded him of the young girl he had flirted with in the Baptist church before the war.

"She's beautiful," Jeff whispered.

"She is," Cry nodded.

"I told you I aimed to marry her," Jeff whispered again.

"I remember..."

And then three men in partial gray uniforms approached on horses, cavalry mounts, at full speed. They brushed Chastity as they passed and she fell. They came on at full speed, passing Cry's father and mother, Jeff's father and mother, and Chastity's mother.

"Lord help us!" the minister cried out.

The young man on the lead horse drew up his mount. It reared and the man fired his pistol three times then turned his mount and raced down the hill, lying low in the saddle to make himself less of a target, but Cry's guns were on his mount beneath the towering oak twenty yards from where he was, bent over Jeff, dead on the ground.

Chastity's screams echoed through the valley as she bent over Jeff, looking into Cry's eyes when she glanced up. Her look betrayed her killer. Cry ran to his horse and raced after the men, wishing Forrest was not in New York, grazing with mares.

Chapter 5

Cry, lying on the deck of the steamship, his head resting on his saddle, grieved. He knew where he was headed. His only hope, more a wish in fact, was that Chastity's lover would go home. He believed he would arrive before the three men. On horseback, believing no one to be in pursuit, Cry felt as though they believed themselves to be safe. He had taken the rails and now the steamboat. He would buy a horse when the boat docked in Missouri. His anger was reserved for the shooter. If he had to deal with all three men, he would. He fell asleep...

"Lay hands suddenly on no man..."

"Who are you?" Cry asked, sitting up as the man knelt beside him.

"Drink no longer water, but use a little wine for your stomach's sake and your often infirmities," the man said, extending a bottle toward Cry.

"No thanks," Cry said.

"Some men's sins are open beforehand, going before to judgment; and some men they follow after as you do these men..."

"Are you a preacher?" Cry asked.

"Even the devil can quote scripture when it is to his advantage, sir. Drink! Drink deeply! I can help you, son. I promise you. Tell me—would you rather kill the one you seek or find the woman?"

Cry did not answer.

"I would let you drive my chariot. You know what it will cost you though, son... Don't you?"

"Yes," Cry said, thinking: *even in dreams the devil is that evil force to be reckoned with...*

As though meaning to plant a seed into Cry's thoughts, the voice in his dream continued saying, "Lincoln was not meant to be born. I told the Indian, who shot his grandfather in the head, to creep up on that boy and kill him. He hesitated. Mordecai, the brother, killed him. Sometimes I lose. Sometimes I win. I lost twice with Lincoln. His mother was illegitimate. I didn't mean for her to be born. She married that boy, Thomas. Your president believed in fate until he went to Gettysburg then he became a Christian."

Cry woke. The hairs on his arms stood up...

Unable to sleep, he thought about Jeff; he thought about Lincoln and Mrs. Lincoln. The only time he had met her, she was grieving. She said: *I understand you lost a horse, one of Clay's stock. I used to walk over to Ashland, Clay's estate, when I was a girl in Lexington and ask if he was willing to see me yet. Once I got there in time for dessert. They gave me a frosted bowl of ice cream. You see, the Clay's had an ice house. They could eat ice cream all year long...*

Chapter 6

"Ho, cuzen!"

Cry turned to face a man and a woman. The man rushed toward him, his hand held out. Cry shook it, pleased with the way Ganaway applied pressure.

"This hyar's the man what sent me down the river, Celia. Martin Kreider, this hyar's my wife."

"Pleased to meet you..."

The woman smiled, but there was fear in her eyes.

"What brings you to Missouri?" Ganaway asked.

Cry told him.

Celia frowned, the fear in her eyes more evident.

"I know the young gal," Ganaway said, "and her beau. Whar ya gonna be at dreckly?"

"I'm headed for the livery. I've got to buy a horse," Cry said.

It did not take long for Cry to pick the horse he wanted from the fourteen mounts at the livery. He chose a grey with its right ear chopped off like Rebel's had been. He paid the blacksmith what the man asked without haggling. He bridled the grey, put on the blanket and saddle...

"Cuzen!"

"What can you tell me?" Cry asked.

"Best take that thar saddle off'n the hoss..."

"Why?"

"Ya figgered ta git hyar furst. They done like ya, took rails and boat. Thay tuk the boat ta Montanny Territory early this morning. Nuther boat hedded out soon. Ya ketch it. Go ta Fort Benton and buy uh hoss. The boy's Maw sed he is gonna see the Guvnur in Montanny..."

Cry removed his tack from the grey.

"He's a good horse," Cry said to Ganaway. "You need him?"

Ganaway did not answer.

"He's yours if you want him."

"I owe ya too metch a ready," Ganaway said.

"Nobody in this town would talk to me," Cry said. "You don't owe me anything. I didn't send you down the Cumberland to obligate you. You're sending me up the Missouri. Peers to me we're even, cuzen."

"I'll take the hoss, Martin. Least wise that way I'll allays owe ya. That's how hit's got ta be. Take care..."

"I will... You do the same, Ganaway..."

"I best meet Celia. She went down thar ta the mill ta git sum uh that new Patent flour she heared about."

"Give her my regards," Cry said.

"I shore nuff will, Cry. Ya best ketch that boat..."

Chapter 7

When Cry entered the Governor's office in Virginia City, he recognized the man seated behind an oak desk. Thomas Meagher had been a Brigadier-General of volunteers from New York.

"Cry!" the Governor shouted. "Come in here! Sit! Sit! Tell me what brings you here! I wouldn't have thought of you for a pewter button."

"It's been a while since you went off with Sherman and I followed Pap to Nashville."

"That it has, Cry. That it has... You know I served the Army as a U. S. citizen. I raised my own company..."

"The Irish Brigade," Cry said.

"We were in the thick of it from May 1862 until May 1863. I raised that brigade myself in New York, you know?"

"General Thomas said it had to be one of the best brigades in the whole war, Governor..."

"Call me Thomas, Cry. Your Pap never saw them fight from Fair Oaks to Mechanicsville—from Gaines' Mill and Peach Orchard to Antietam—from Fredericksburg to Chancellorsville. I watched them—led them—watched them die, 3,500 of the 4,000 in my command. For him to say what he said makes me proud. I believe him to be the best general of the war. After I had resigned because I was refused my request to recruit more men to fill the ranks of my decimated brigade and after they called me back to serve in the western armies, I wanted to serve with General Thomas. Instead, you know where I went..."

"With General Sherman..."

"The man called me a rabble-rouser and made me a military administrator to get me out of his hair. I supervised the military occupation of Savannah, Georgia of all things. I saw your father in Washington. We paid our last respects to Lincoln at the same time. I asked about you..."

"You know what I think of Sherman..."

"And Grant, too... I know... At least Sherman's a converted Catholic. Grant is still Commander of the U. S. Army and will be President. He has given General Sherman the assignment of dealing with the Plains Indians to make way for railroads."

"I pity them," Cry said.

"Sherman told me the same thing that he told Grant..."

"What?"

"Said we are not going to let a few thieving, ragged Indians check and stop progress of the railroads or slow down expansion...I don't want to appear to be too busy to treat you like I should, but I am overwhelmed at the moment. Indian tribes want the miners out. Miners want the Army in so they can get the Black Hills gold. I need guns. I might need for you to help with that. Tell me what the General needs..."

"It's not Pap, sir," Cry said. "It's personal..."

"Let's hear it..."

Cry told him...

Chapter 8

When Cry got off the train in Louisville, he gave the man behind the desk at the passenger station a gold dollar to send a telegram and watch his saddle until he returned. From the passenger station at 9th and Broadway, he normally would have made his way toward the Galt House, the best-known hotel in the city. To his surprise Governor Meagher had told him not to go to First and Market, for there was only an empty lot where the hotel had been. The Galt House had burned.

He went to a new hotel on Main Street and found no one on duty in the lobby. He sat down in the only chair with an unobstructed view of the street. As he suspected, a man who had followed him from the passenger station, entered the hotel.

"I thought you knew I was following you, Cry," the man said, extending his hand.

Cry did not shake hands with him.

"Jeff was my friend," the man said, his hand still held toward Cry who shook it after those words.

"How did you know Jeff?" he asked.

"We worked for the same man..."

"Pap?"

"I came from Nashville yesterday. General Thomas is doing a hell of a job there. He said for me to tell you to come back to work as soon as you've finished your business."

"He doesn't need me now," Cry said.

"He said to tell you that he has discovered a secret society called the Ku Klux Klan that aims to restore white supremacy and resist Reconstruction in the South. He expects it will be a force to be reckoned with. Word has it that Forrest is high up in its organization. I told him I'd tell you before I offered you Jeff's position..."

"I'm not looking for a job."

"I understand that, Cry. Do you know what bill President Lincoln signed on April 14, his final act as president?"

"I'm not sure," Cry stated.

"He created his own Secret Service, a branch of the Treasury Department whose mission it is to combat counterfeiting of U.S. currency."

"That was a good move on his part..."

"Do you play chess?"

"When I was at school," Cry answered, "I played often..."

"Jeff taught me. He was not just a friend, Cry. He was my best friend."

A tear formed in Cry's right eye...

"He talked about you all the time..."

"Then you understand why I'm not interested in working with you," Cry said.

"I know you understand how wartime inflation drove the gold value of the Union greenback to 46¢ and reduced the value of Confederate paper money to $1.70 per $100 by the end of the war."

"I'd say the greenback won't regain its full value for some time..."

"We worked for the First head of the Secret Service, a veteran named William P. Wood."

"I know Bill," Cry said. "He slipped behind enemy lines on many occasions to gain information for us before he was sent to Washington as commandant of the Capitol Prison."

"Mr. Wood brought us on at the same time, July 1 when nearly one third of Union currency was counterfeit. His order to us, as agents of the Treasury Department, was simple: that our chief responsibility was detecting and bringing to trial and punishment, persons engaged in counterfeiting treasury notes, bonds, and other securities of the United States."

"I hope they pay you better than they paid the soldiers..."

"We started out at $3 per day and Jeff was earning $5. He broke a counterfeiting ring, a small operation, in August."

"You'll find someone for that kind of money," Cry assured him.

"I have to have a man like Jeff, like you, one who recognizes his service belongs to the government 24 hours of each day."

"I'm not your man."

"You have proved yourself to be otherwise," the man said. "Your fitness is beyond question. Jeff was a great investigator, with honesty and fidelity in all transactions."

"I'm on the trail of three men..."

"I know. I found them last night. They're in room 312," the man said. "I have to tell you... you can't touch them..."

"I know they're part of the Fenian movement, but I aim to kill one of them," Cry said.

"I don't know much about that secret society," the man confessed.

"The Irish Republican Brotherhood," Cry said. "My mother is Irish. She sends funds to Stephens and the IRB in her hometown. She wants Britain to give Ireland its independence as badly as any member of the Fenian Brotherhood in this country wants freedom..."

"Mr. Wood has set his sights on a notorious currency counterfeiter, William Brockaway, and he will get him, but you won't get the men who killed Jeff..."

Cry did not tell the man what he believed, thinking: *most of the Fenians served in the Army of the Cumberland. I know them. They knew Jeff. The three men fought us.*

"Here," Cry said, handing the man a Fenian Button, one of two his mother had given him the morning of Jeff's death.

The man took it; examined it and said," Neatly made..."

"It's not counterfeit," Cry smiled. "If you follow the *Morning Herald* or *The Cork Examiner*, you know they predict an outbreak in Ireland this winter. Ireland is full of returned emigrants from America, reckless, but first-rate soldiers..."

"I don't follow those papers, but I understand that there are ships at sea loaded with arms and ammunitions, and many fighting men..."

"You say Jeff was your friend..."

"My best friend," the man repeated.

"That was Jeff's button. You keep it. Now get out of here!"

The man put the button in his vest pocket and turned to go, turning back toward Cry after he had taken four steps...

"I don't need to know your name," Cry told him and turned away, moving toward the door to the right of the lobby desk where a man stood, looking up the stairs.

Chapter 9

Cry knocked on the door of room 312. He waited but no one came to open it; no one called out an inquiry from inside. He knocked again rapidly and stepped to the right so he could kick the door. He drew his pistols and waited until the door began to open slowly. He kicked swiftly with his left foot and lunged forward. The man who had answered the door fell backward, recovered quickly, raising his arms...

"Hell! Don't shoot, Cry! It's me, John Hoy."

"John!"

Laughter rang out from the back of the room. Cry counted six men, standing. He saw the three men he sought, gagged and bound, sitting on chairs between the double beds.

"I think you know Bailey, Stagg, McCovey, Lynch, and Mooney," John said.

"I do," Cry said. "I don't recognize the young man with his hands in his pockets.

"That's Edward Lonergan, ship's carpenter. He's not armed. Put those guns away, Cry."

"I came for them," Cry said, pointing his Navy Colt at the man in the middle, the man who had killed Jeff. "Let me have him, Colonel Stagg..." Cry said to the man in the group that he knew best.

"I'm sorry, Cry," the man, who had commanded the 78th New York Volunteers, said, moving forward. "You can't have him or them."

As if by prior order, five men pulled their pistols and pointed them at Cry.

"You aim to kill me, Henry?"

"No," the man said, positioning himself between Cry and the man from Missouri. "We aim to kill them, but not here."

"Take the two on the ends and leave me with the one in the middle..."

"Won't do that," Henry said. "You aim to kill me?"

"I mean to kill him!"

"Your uncle wants to see him die, Cry. He's headed here by rail from Cincinnati. Your mother asked us to do this... We'd never go against you otherwise! Besides, Jeff was only your cousin; he was the man's son. Put your arms aside..."

"You got here first," Cry said, looking around the room at the men, unflinching, "with the most as Forrest would say..."

"Promise us you won't hold this against us," John Hoy said.

"I won't come looking for you, John," Cry said, holstering his Colts.

Chapter 10

Cry moved from the present tense, from the now of seeking revenge for Jeff's murder when he saw his uncle step off the train and rush ahead of the others to meet John Hoy.

The past returned. It was not gone—not best forgotten. He knew, in that moment, the war was over for him. The awareness of it would, however—and he had no doubts about it—shape the future, for him, for his family, for Pap—he turned, facing south, and saluted, for his uncle for whom the recent past was still happening until he could come face to face with the three men, but most of all, Cry realized, for the nation, not European or Eastern with histories rooted in antiquity. He understood that war-torn and divided America had only been born yesterday and reborn yesterday when it became today.

Now, he thought, *I can go back.*

The memories, those of Alyx, that he had repressed but had not been able to dismiss—those memories that would not stay down or out of his mind's sight—he could face at once...

"Sir?"

Cry turned.

"I'll get my saddle now," Cry said to the man from the passenger station.

"It's behind my counter, but I saw you standing here deep in thought and I figured I needed to get you this... It came back not long after I sent yours..."

With his right hand, Cry took the telegram, and with his left hand dug for another gold dollar, but when he offered the coin, the man shook his head and began to walk away.

Son, Cry read: **come home at once. Mom...**

Chapter 11

Cry whistled and Forrest left the mares, running as he approached the whitewashed, wooden fence that ran from the front of the house to the barn.

"Did you forget me, old man?" Cry asked.

The horse pawed the ground and twitched his ears.

"I brought you one," Cry said, extending his left hand and a slice of an apple that he had quartered.

Cry watched the stallion for a moment then remembered how right he had been when he got his mother's telegram. Her message had told him, as surely as a dreaded knock on the door in the early hours before dawn plants dread in the heart of the awakened, that some tragedy had struck his family.

Cry turned suddenly when his mother put her hand on his shoulder. He had not heard her approach.

"Sorry," he said.

"Don't be, son," she answered. "It will be a splendid wake, won't it?"

"Father was a good man," he said, "and well liked..."

"That he was. He left this place to you, and the horses, but I can't let you keep Forrest..."

Cry looked at her. Tears flowed freely.

"That thoroughbred's all I've got left of your father's love. He loved that horse. He knew you loved him, too. You should have him, but he'll be what keeps me thinking about you when I am in Ireland."

"I can't say no to you, you know?"

"Neither could your father. I married him when I was sixteen and he was almost twenty. In that time, he never said no to me. There were many times I felt guilty..."

"You didn't have to," Cry said. "You don't have to go. This is your home..."

"County Kildare has always been my home. I've yearned for it since my parents brought me here when I was fourteen. They died with cholera, too, if you remember the stories..."

"I do."

'Your father just got back from Paris where he met my brother, your uncle Patrick whom you've never met. You will have to come visit us..."

"Perhaps I will..."

"Promise me..."

"I promise," Cry said, for he meant it.

She saw what she had wanted to see and smiled.

"Promise me you won't give all your money to the IRB..."

"Your father took them the last of the money that they will ever ask of me," she said. "You've had enough war, son, or I'd ask you to help us."

"Getting the British out will take longer than anyone in Kildare or Cork, or Dublin imagines..."

"You could be right," she said, "but I am yet young..."

"And beautiful," Cry said.

"With these puffy, red eyes?" she asked.

"Beautiful," he said.

"After Newbridge, on the main road from Dublin to the south, pasture land turns into a high plain dotted with gorse bushes. It is beautiful, son, more beautiful than any woman. When I was ten, I would walk from our farm early enough to watch the strings of thoroughbreds get put through their daily exercise. Kildare is the county of the horse. It has always been and always will be."

"You never talked about such things before..."

"I used to love the auctions in the village of Kill. The owners of the stud farms were rich, of Anglo-Irish descent. I always begged Father to buy me a horse. We were poor, but we had land. Patrick lives on it. There is a cottage by the barn. My money will be put to good use, on repairs, but I won't have to buy a stallion. That Kentucky bred," she pointed at Forrest. "He is beautiful."

"He is a winner," Cry said.

"He will cover many mares," his mother said.

"How many of the mares are with foal?"

"Four," she said. "Let's go celebrate your father's life..."

Chapter 12

The wake, the celebration that Cry and his mother joined, was lively, musicians, a guitarist, a pianist, and a violinist played while his father's friends, their wives and children, danced, ate, and drank.

The ritual was Irish as were those, for the most part, who had come for the funeral. Cry had attended five wakes that he could remember. He felt out of place at each of them, and more German because of his father. It was during the third that he learned from an Irish jockey whose name he had long since forgotten that the wake began in Irish culture during a time when drinking mugs were full of lead, in the clay itself and in the paint and sealant used to decorate them. He had not forgotten, however, the man's narrative about lead poisoning.

Lead poisons a man slowly he had said. *A man dies because he drinks lead, God's punishment for transgression against one of his divine laws. Too much beer or wine kills a man only until he sleeps off his stupor. A man, woman, young or old who dies from lead poisoning, may not be dead, only in a stupor. My Irish father knew that as did a thousand years of Irish mothers who told stories of men, women, and children buried alive, only to revive in a casket beneath the dirt. We experience death only as observers. As watchers, it is our duty to set up with the dead, to stay awake in case life returns. If life returns, there should be merry making all around, not tears.*

At midnight, Alden Goldsmith stood by the casket in silence for a few moments. The musicians stopped playing. The dancing, the drinking, the eating ceased...

"Kreider, true friend," Alden said, "I bought the mare, the trotter you wanted, the one you said would make money at New Jersey harness tracks for her owner. I call her Goldsmith Mare, for she has not yet earned a name. If I had known this, I would have called her Kreider's Mare. You know how she ran wild as a colt. No one can break her yet. I raced her at Goshen. She was eight, untamed, but she ran. Nothing can come close to her when she takes the bits. She is a runaway no doubt about it. I drink this toast to you, old friend: may every race she runs find you looking on..."

When the man drank the beer and returned to his chair, the musicians played, other toasts, silent ones, were made, and dancing resumed.

At three in the morning, Cry's mother stood by the casket in silence. The studio, space enough for a full-orchestra, grew quiet. After a time, she turned to face the onlookers.

"I've told myself all my life the best I can do is struggle against death as though it is my final enemy. I never imagined that the man I adore would die. I never imagined I would want to feel what death means to me by looking at my fantasies, but that is what I have done. I have always imagined that I would die in Ireland. When I leave here, I will go home to die. Do not read into my moving some sinister death wish I have harbored for this man. He did not die the way he expected. If he could have had his way, he would have died at a racetrack or in a paddock while trainers and owners parade their horses. Who dies so young? My parents, and soldiers, as we know too well, but my Martin—never could you have made me believe that he would...He did not die to make room for the living. He did not die because his body was worn out. In death, he does not wear a mask of tragedy or deliverance. He was no man's enemy so he does not wear the mask of retribution or justice. He who gave me my greatest pleasure is dead. This is my greatest sorrow. It is a strangeness I cannot explain."

Chapter 13

His mother and Forrest were on a ship bound for Ireland two days after his father was buried on a knoll where fruit trees grew. The knoll was half way between the house and the horse barn. Cry had let a contract to a carpenter for an iron fence to surround the base of the small rise and he, and two jockeys, Santos and David, had buried a gas line from the house to the foot of his father's grave...

"May I?" Santos asked, holding a lantern.

"Certainly," Cry said, reaching a candle toward him. "And one for you, too, David."

The man smiled.

Cry turned the valve and there was no sound, no smell of natural gas for several minutes.

"Now," Cry told them when he heard the hiss.

It was a calm evening. The jockeys, in their green silks, lit their candles from the lantern's wick and then lit the burner.

His father had invested in oil wells in 1864 after a *finder* using a witch-hazel twig divining rod discovered petroleum along Pennsylvania's Pithole Creek. Pithole Creek, a hamlet made headlines when oil drillers brought in a gusher there in January of the next year. The well was soon pumping 250 barrels of oil per day, and by the end of June four wells at the new town of Pithole pumped more than 2,000 barrels per day, one-third of all the oil produced in Pennsylvania.

His father sold his interest in two wells when the price of petroleum rose to $12.00 per barrel. Drillers, business agents, speculators, and hangers-on poured into Pithole as his father left. He had the foresight to get out of the oil business when producers began to explode gunpowder deep inside wells to increase their yields, and before a glut of oil drove the price down dramatically. Jeff had told him the news when they met in Nashville before he set out to find Bedford and learn from him where to look for the stallion, Forrest.

After he returned to New York, his father had convinced a water well driller to put down a hole behind their house in search of petroleum. Although they did not strike oil, there was gas enough in the well to be capped and used. The gas from the wellhead furnished lights for the house throughout the year and fuel to heat it in winter.

After the first day of battle at Nashville, Cry had helped gather the wounded as night fell upon the battlefield. It was the first time he had seen a hand cranked Gatlin gun in use on a battlefield. It was also the first time he had driven an ambulance.

On his third trip to pick up the wounded, one of Steedman's Negro soldier's asked Cry to bury him with his face to the east, the direction from which the new day is born, and with two canteens of water in his coffin for the long journey he would make. He also wanted a repeating rifle, for he had never shot one. He begged Cry, after the dirt got mounded above him, to pile wood at his feet and set fire to it that it might cast light upon the darkness of his grave.

Cry had done those things for the young man. He wished now that he had asked the dying soldier his name, for when the flame flickered he would have dedicated the flame to both his father and the black youth.

"Who was the woman at the barn?" Cry asked.

The men did not answer.

"The woman?" Cry asked again. "She should have come with you to the grave..."

"She is a woman from the brothel beyond the tracks, Cry," David, holding his head down, finally answered.

Chapter 14

Before she left, taking Forrest with her as she had said she would, his mother had given him a key to his father's trunk, one his family had brought with them from the mountains of Switzerland. He had not opened it. He thought he would, but he did not go directly to his father's library. He had not slept at all; his thoughts haunted by his father, by Jeff, and by Alyx, who, he told himself, could also be dead...

The man at the passenger station in Louisville could not have been Alyx he said to himself.

In the hours before dawn while he stood by the window looking from the bedroom to the knoll where the flame cast a bright light upon the ground, he wondered whether his looking inside for answers was but a futile search.

He decided that he still believed in love, for his mother's conversation before the wake had showed him that her love for his father was real. He had not been one to believe the romantic stories that he heard before the war. With Alyx, as they traveled upriver, there had been an attraction he had not been able to deny, but he could not say it was love. The closest thing it could have been, he decided, was the hope of love...

Attraction and happiness do not go hand in hand... he thought.

He remembered a story his father had told after returning from Ireland. He said that: *two men were passing along the water's edge one night when a great snake raised its huge head, then its body to a height of ten feet. The snake flung a stream of venom at them. It missed. The men swore to him that the snake was thirty feet long, with a mane like a horse almost ten feet long. Its mouth was big enough to swallow a hog.* Then his father had lunged at him and, being young, he screamed... Remembering, he smiled and looked out the window again.

He saw a figure at the head of his father's grave. He dressed quickly and left the house by the back door.

Chapter 15

"You should have come..."

"Shit!" the woman cried out. "Scared the hell out of me, you did!"

"Sorry," Cry said. "I just wanted to tell you that you should have come over from the barn with Santos and David..."

"I couldn't do that for your mother's sake," the woman said. "Do you know what I am?"

"I can see that you are a woman..."

"I haven't been a woman in years, Cry..."

"You know my name?"

"I was your father's first," she said. "I've kept up with him, with his family, all these years."

"He told me about you..."

"He did?" she asked.

He told her the story.

"I'm Jane," the woman said. "He was younger than you are... Younger than I was. He was so kind. I've spent all these years wanting someone like him to come and take me away. Why is sex such a hard thing for us to understand?"

"You're asking the wrong guy, Jane..."

She chuckled.

"You've come home with your legs and your arms, Cry. There are countless young women who hope you will come into their lives. You can pick any number of them for love or lust. They will have sex with you, hoping to marry you."

"I saw my cousin killed by a man who wanted the woman he was about to marry. Jeff died not knowing why he was gunned down. Besides, I can't get a woman off my mind..."

"Then keep her there," Jane said. "I have held your father in my dreams all these years; sometimes my arms around him, but mostly empty without him. I lost any sense of who I am along the way. Believe me, I have asked myself why I am in this world at all."

"You are the only person I have met who understands my pain..."

"No, Cry, I only understand my own. When all is said and done, nothing will matter. Love is a crazy thing..."

"Sometimes I tell myself it is insanity."

"My quest was not for pleasure, but for the money I had to have to survive, and for intimacy. I know that as sure as I stand here. I only regret that he died first. My wish was to die after he left that morning, but now I have only a short time left. The hazards of my profession, Cry. I'd like to be buried at your father's feet... I'd like for my tombstone to say: *a friend...* Nothing else..."

It was a request that Cry could not deny...

Chapter 16

Cry went to bed. He tried to sleep, but sleeping came hard, for he lay wide-eyed awake, thinking...

Once, when he was younger, his father came into his room after he had ridden a new mare, one that took the bits and ran through the wooden fence with him, for he had been unable to stop or turn her. She broke her leg. He rode her to the ground and got off unhurt but had to go find his father, carrying guilt as though it were a burlap bag filled with corn.

He could hear his father's voice, saying: *Son, if you are overcome by what happened, it is time for you to sleep. When you sleep, someone or something can come to you and give you power over your misfortune or give you an understanding of it. In your dreams, listen, see everything, and learn what is expected of you.*

He had dreamed that night, and in the dream, a foal came to him and nibbled at his fingers. The next morning, he asked his father to go with him to a neighboring farm where there would be an auction. When the auctioneer had sold the livestock except for a mare and her foal, they were brought into the corral. The foal came to him and nibbled at his fingers. It was as if his dream had been a flash from the future. He bought the mare and her colt with his money he had earned selling plow points, handles, single trees and trace chains at the warehouse. He gave them to his father. The mare, first of the herd bred to Forrest, was that colt from his dream and from the auction...

He fell asleep thinking about Alyx. He dreamed.

Alyx lying on her back, naked on white sheets, did not hear him approach her bed. She did not move as he blew out the lamp and crawled next to her. In the darkness, she glowed. He longed to touch her; ached with desire; burned with longing; knew he had to kiss her. When he moved to touch her, putting his left hand between her legs, fingers were there, not his, not hers, but fingers and strong hands...

He pulled back his hand, afraid to touch her again. When he tried to touch her, feel her as he thought a lover would, four hands, women's hands, illuminated like Alyx was, appeared. He reached across Alyx, fear telling him to shake her until she opened her eyes. A hand caught his arm. He tried to move closer to Alyx but the other three hands came between them.

The hands were powerful; they were soft. He realized that they were not threatening him. The hand with his left arm placed it at his side and took his right arm and bent it above and around Alyx's head and the three hands pushed his body up, bending his head toward her bare shoulder—into the bend of her neck. He kissed her softly and the hands did not interfere. The three hands moved, disappeared, and he was naked, his body cool against her warm skin.

He moved his left arm, softly placing his hand upon her stomach and inching his fingers down, down. For the second time, he could not touch her where he sought. A hand covered her and two hands lifted his arm, placing it gently upon her breast while a hand beneath his chin pushed his head upward until his lips touched skin beneath her ear.

Alyx turned her face toward him without waking and he kissed her. The hands would not leave him and he gave himself to them until he was daring, but never dangerous—until he could feel without thinking—until he could touch without hesitating and speak without words.

The hands led him through his new found knowledge to her secret places. And when he was not afraid of her body, they went away. He knew, in that moment, that he had always been looking for her—had always been destined to be her knight.

Chapter 17

After his father's attorney read the will, Cry drew up a contract for David and Santos, outlining their duties in his absence, for he meant to be gone until he found Alyx.

When Cry came home from the city, he went to his father's library and opened the trunk. Inside was a letter from his father. He read it slowly.

Son,

I know I will not be alive when next you are in New York. Women fill hope chests before they marry. In a sense, you might consider this a hope chest, for I pray you use its contents to find the slave girl.

When I was in Paris, I visited the Louvre and I saw an oil on canvas by Willem Drost. The moment I saw it, I thought it was a painting you have to see. I hope you get to Paris in your lifetime. It was a scene of a woman, Bathsheba. The strangest feeling came over me that the model wasn't a stranger—not to you, as she was to me... I decided the vibes came from the slave girl. Call me insane if you must, but I thought that—felt that....

The first money belt you gave me, as well as the last one you sent to me by Jeff, you will find inside this trunk. I did not have to use the gold in them to buy arms. I was able to raise money from many interested parties. You cannot imagine how much more steel was worth when I smelted the John Deere plowshares we had on hand at the warehouse and had them pounded into swords.

Beneath this letter is a book I want you to read. I found it in Ohio when I was looking for your girl. I found no hint of her in the Underground Railroad safe houses of Cincinnati or Covington or in Maysville, but I met a young woman in Ohio who was introduced to me as Thomas Jefferson's granddaughter. If your girl is anything like she is, I can imagine how beautiful she must be. The book, Clotel; or The President's Daughter, is a first edition by William Wells Brown. The owner of the bookstore where I purchased it insisted it is one of the first African American novels published in the States. Its story supports the young lady's claim as to her lineage. I believe your cousin Jeff's namesake fell in love with and fathered children by his slave. I would not say that to anyone in the Jefferson family, and I hope you will not either. I write this for your eyes and yours alone...

Before I sent you to Nashville, you were the quietest of young men. I cannot recall ever seeing you angry, though you were sometimes irritated when matters went wrong at the stables. I trust your love of horses has not been dampered by my scheme. If I put you in a position where you could have sex with a woman, I thought you would take on a new manner, one of talking more, for I am and have always been, a man of conversation. We know how foolish I was.

At home, not only were you quiet, but also, you were happy. I don't believe I ever saw you unhappy until I came to Lexington and brought you home. At least, I know I never saw you unhappy for any length of time before your terrible ordeal.

I sent you to school, hoping you would study engineering, for I could see that you had but little taste or care for agricultural pursuits or farm machinery sales. Knowing that, I suggest that you put matters pertaining to the farm mostly with stewards that are trustworthy. I would suggest Santos and David, but you might find others as equally dependable if you take time to advertise the position(s). I also suggest that you offer your Uncle the overseer's position. I would like to know that Mary is home. Nashville will not be home for them. It has not been since the war. I never had the chance to thank you for fixing their house. It looked great. I know they planned to give it to Jeff and Chastity. I know they can't live there. I told them to sell it and bring Jeff up here. If they do, put him at my head. You might think that I am being morbid, but I am not. I am dying as I write. I feel life leaving me. I realize at this moment that I can only experience dying. You, your mother, and my closest friends must experience death as your Aunt and Uncle have.

I imagine you are restless. You took to war, not as a soldier, but as—whatever it was that you became. Some say you were a spy. Some called you a sniper. Jeff said you were General Thomas' most secret weapon. The General is a remarkable man. We talked after the Mills Spring battle when I came to see if I could get you to come home. You were delivering the mail.. That one time, I liked him. From what you have said of him, never taking one day off during the war, teaching the slaves to read when he was young, hiring the first woman doctor ever to work with his wounded and riding on the shoulder of the road so his men could pass— he has outstanding qualities for a soldier...

I told you the woman I first made love to was older than me. She was, by less than two years. I have seen her all these years past. Life has been harder on her than it was to your mother, probably in Ireland as you read this. May God protect her! The woman, Jane, was a mistake my father made. I fear she felt things for me that I could not feel for her. If that is so, I regret it. If it is not so, it is this dying man's shame, one that began to gnaw at me when you spent a year here trying to live when I was convinced that you would die.

I do not regret, as I take my final breaths, however, my attempt at providing you your first woman. I understand you did not know her as David knew Bathsheba, or the young man who killed Jeff knew Chastity. Yes, I knew. Her father told me before the ceremony. He begged me to tell Jeff, but I chose not to... Perhaps we should have told him, you and I, son, but we wanted him to be happy. Chastity told me you knew as well. She begged me to find you, but I chose not to follow after you. I hope your mother's friends found you before you found him—them. Your mother has your abilities, son. Of all the things in this world, I shall miss my Julie most.

I am proud of you...

There is a bundle at the bottom of the chest. A high-spirited, young man who missed you at the passenger station in Louisville gave it to me. After I told him you were my son and he had missed his train, I gave him a key to Jeff's room so he might compose it while he waited for the next train north. I do hope it is not a letter you should have received immediately. I had it with me at Nashville and meant to give it to you after the ceremony. Since that day, you have been on your quest for the man who gunned down Jeff. Know this: I have not read it.

I am,

Your Father

Chapter 18

Cry emptied the chest to get to the bundle at the bottom. As he began to remove the white ribbons that bound it, there was a knock at the front door...

He put the bundle on the floor beside the book and the money belts then went to the parlor.

"Santos," Cry asked, "what's wrong?"

"They have brought Jeff," the jockey said. "Where shall we put him?"

"At my father's head," Cry said. "Tell them that is where he wants him... Tell them I'll be right out..."

"Take your time," Santos said. "We'll be digging for a while."

"I just need to put away a few things and then I'll help."

"No need for that," Santos said.

"Yes," Cry said. "Send David to fetch Reverend Sweeney..."

Journeys

Book Four

A Letter, a Map & a Palm Reader

Chapter 1

Cry unpacked the trunk; took out the bundle; removed the string; glanced at the map, then put it aside; unwrapped the letter and began to read:

Cry,

I don't know where to begin. You are alive! I never expected... Never thought... I gave this to your father... Actually, I was trying to get to you as you got on the train to return to Nashville. I shouted your name.

Your father heard me; came to me; introduced himself and I told him my name was Alyxander. I told him I met you in Creelsboro. I told him how you won a race there and he said he had no idea... That told me you have been caught up in this war. I asked about the stallion. He said you have not found him. Perhaps you shall... Then he told me how he arranged for you to buy the horse and the Fancy Gal. He told me what he had planned for you... with her or me, I suppose...

Your father told me he would be in Louisville for three days, waiting for your cousin to return from near the Tennessee line and waiting to get a telegram from someone at Nashville about the battle that would be fought there... He seemed to be worried. Now, I worry about you. He told me to walk with him to the Museum Hotel on Main Street where I could use your cousin's room to write this letter to you. I'm sure he never expected me to write so much. I didn't expect to ramble like I am... I took him up on his offer...

I'm in the room as I write this, but all I can see is you falling into the mud, shot outside Berea. What a nightmare Berea turned out to be...for both of us... I rode behind that man with those scissors you dropped, waiting for my chance to use them. It is amazing that I had my grandmother's dagger in my boot. What is more amazing is the fact that no man who owned me ever saw it but you.

We rode hard toward the river, Rockcastle, and the mare tried to cross the stream first. The stallion must have picked up her scent and read it for what it was, for he reared, mounted her, and I got my chance. I buried the scissors in the man's left shoulder just behind his collar bone and slid down into that cold water. I swam downstream.

I started back toward you, but the man did not die. He came after me, staggering. I ran as fast as I could and when I got out of sight, I turned back toward the river. The horses were gone. I thought I had saved your stallion, but it turns out that I did not accomplish even that...

I hid like a fawn until nightfall. When the moon rose, I decided to cross the river. I felt like I would be safer in Mt. Vernon. The man bragged that Berea would never be a school again, and I had a sick feeling that he was right.

I don't know whether you remember it, but on the Wilderness Road, that white house with the porch across the front on the hillside in Mt. Vernon is where I went. It turned out to be a safe house. The family owned slaves, but they also helped slaves move north to freedom. There were five men at the house when I arrived. At least one of the men at the house must have fathered two children by a slave woman named Fanny. I hid in the cellar for a week by myself. Fanny brought my meals, but she never talked with me. I began to realize that she was jealous of me for being so white. I figured that out from her actions. One man came down with her the second morning and each morning after that. I could tell he wanted me. I also knew that I would be raped again when Fanny finally talked. All she said was that I was whiter than she was and the men talked about it every other word. Then she told me three of the men had drawn lots for me. I knew I was in for more scars, the kind that get cut across the soul. I told her I had had enough of kidnapping and being sold into slavery. I decided I would be raped when they moved us north to hide out at the Clay mansion. I did not tell her I planned to leave before morning, but the man who won me, not the man who first came down with Fanny, came down where I was in the middle of the night. He raped me before we left, the seven of us; the two other men from the north, him, Fanny, her two children, a girl and a boy, and me. Fanny wanted to chat as we traveled, but one of the men shushed her. I knew the other men were eager to take their turns with me.

I got the chance to run when we approached the river and I took it. I have not regretted that, for I ran west, always away from the morning sun and toward the evening sun. I got home if you can believe that. There was no one in the house where I was born. I was a queen in a valley of shadows, but I loved it until I realized that I was with child.

When I found out, I screamed and cursed the Lord. I cried unlike I had ever cried before. I kept telling myself that it couldn't be real. After everything that I had been through the last thing I needed was a child. I could not help thinking that , I, myself was a mere child.

It was not long before I began to think rationally as my Memaw had taught me. It was as though her voice came to me, saying: **this is in the hand of a greater power than you. Everything will come to be as it is supposed to be.**

There I was pregnant and basically alone without any idea of what to do next. I had never really been around children in the sense of caring for an infant. Memaw and ma could have told me what to expect, what to do and they would have held me while I cried.

I kept denying it, for I wanted to be free, not burdened by this thing that seemed so unreal. It seemed as impossible for it to be true as it would have been for me to have crawled on top of myself and got myself in this fix. Reality hit me when my body started changing and I started to grow. I grew very slowly and if there had been family there with me, most of them would not have even noticed. I tried to hide it and did for a few months. There were only birds, an old fox that hid in the canes by the river, squirrels with eyes to see me, and Old Bess, our family milk cow. She had a wild bull with her, probably her own calf. She came right up to me and I milked her in a crock. In a few days, she brought home a bull calf and a springer heifer. I slaughtered the calf. The heifer was too wild to handle but she dropped a bull calf and I found it at the head of the hollow and led old Bess up to it. It followed her to the barn and she raised it for she gave enough milk for it and still had enough for me to churn butter. She had survived all those years since we were sold. I don't know why she was not sold, but, for me, she was a symbol of survival, and, better yet, of freedom...

Oh, but I knew there was a child. I could tell the minute things started to change that my body was going to be different. I smiled one morning when I remembered how you measured my hips and told me I shouldn't want wide hips like my sisters' had. I understood the truth in your words. The changes in my body were hard for me. I had never struggled with such thoughts before, but in my mind, I felt ugly. I never felt really pretty after those young men raped me the first time, but I knew how to get attention with my body. You know that. I had your attention. Seems like most of the time it turned out to be unwanted attention and some man or men would have their way with me.

My Memaw would have said that is the price we pay for our sins. I never wanted such sins. I never wanted to be a slave. It is a miracle that I wasn't killed for what I said to some of those men. I have also realized that because of the abuse inflicted upon my body, whether some might say it was by my own allowance or that of those who abused me against my will, one thing was clear. The child, growing inside my body was a miracle.

That is how I chose to look at the situation. I decided to work, honest and hard, be fair and truthful, and take the best care of my child that I possibly could for as long as there was breath in my body. And that is exactly what I do, Cry.

I wanted to be a doctor. I had you cut my hair and buy me a man's clothes. What good did that do me? I kept telling myself that my foolish notions got you killed. How happy your father made me when he said you survived. I have accepted the fact that earning a living from working the soil is what I know. I realized that after my morning sickness stopped. I set to farming with a vengeance. I worked continuously to make sure I could provide for my baby. I knew that in my situation I would have to work extra hard in order to achieve what would come easier for others, such as you, Cry. I sensed that you were troubled by your lot in life, but you never complained.

In fact, if the truth be known, I worked and stressed so much that I had to put myself on bed rest, being my own midwife, giving myself my own doctor's orders. I don't know how I knew it, but for the last six to eight weeks of my pregnancy, I told myself to do everything I needed to do in an eight hour time frame and the other sixteen hours I forced myself to rest.

In the beginning, this was all fine, however, anxiety caused me to pursue my ritualistic habits and I would cook and clean to occupy my time. I really believe it was to occupy my thoughts much more than my time. I thought I was the smart one by working what I thought to be much less than before and each time I would visit myself as midwife or doctor, one voice or the other would tell me what I was doing and I would have to settle down again.

Even with all my unattended medical complications toward the end, I would dare say one of the hardest parts was the loneliness. How every woman longs to have someone to share the joys of her pregnancy with and I was alone. I felt guilty if I was excited. I would try to convince myself the child was unwanted. I thought to myself: **How can anyone be excited?** *But deep down inside I really was in so many ways. No matter what the circumstances behind the conception, this child was part of me. It got so I realized that it did not really matter who else was involved. I was the one chosen to carry the child and I would soon be a mother. It would be a girl. I knew it in my heart. It just had to be a girl. I rationalized* that God knew that being a young, single mother was hard enough and raising a boy who would some day turn into a man who would probably be like all the other men in the world would just be plain wrong.

I feel so shameful for feeling that way now and I know that I would have loved a son just as much as I do my daughter, but my heart's desire was heard and in the fall I gave birth to the most beautiful little girl I had ever laid eyes on! I labored for sixteen hours. She took her time coming into the world. I believe this was to prepare me for the patience that one must endure whenever they start the journey of motherhood.

And there we were…I held her for what seemed like forever. She had mesmerized my heart and I would never be the same again. I never knew it was possible for a human to love something so entirely, so unconditionally, it is totally indescribable. I later learned that giving birth, well, that is the easy part.

I had to go back to the crops at once. I had to work in order to provide for me and my daughter. But, once again it was not the work that was the hardest, it was the loneliness. I was not alone now, I did have her, but it wasn't the same. In that quiet, undisturbed valley, I learned the truth behind Memaw's saying: **that you can be in a room full of people and still feel so alone inside that you just want to die.**

It was hardest at night. Sometimes I would sing to her until she went to sleep and watch her as I held her asleep. Other times, I would cry myself to sleep and sometimes I would just lie beside her thinking. I had to keep in my mind that I had something wonderful to live for and someone that loved and depended on me.

But many times I thought about you. I thought I had never met such a man. Every man I had ever met wanted me, maybe not permanently, but they wanted me if only for a short time. It was hard for me to think that you might somehow not find me detestable. Then I thought, that's not it, for Cry told me he wanted me various times. I asked myself then why did you not act upon your desires when you knew you could have done whatever you wished with me, a slave girl, property only?

I decided that you must be one of the most moral men alive. I had been with enough men in my life to know that they really have no control over their desires. Those feelings deep inside of a man are innate. Men can't help themselves my Memaw always said. Men are visual creatures by nature. I played on that visual make up of yours. My dressing and undressing in front of you was meant to be so very hard on you. Women know that clothes can hide their imperfections, imagined or real. I wanted you to see me. At first, I hoped my scars would make you pity me. You never pitied me; that I could tell. You wanted to make my rapists pay with their lives. You can't know how that made me feel or how taken back I was when you said you wanted to paint me...

When you were ready to give in, you ran out of the room and I shall never forget how you lamented the fact that I was so beautiful. You may not have understood why I was playing you. You thought I meant to kill you. I thought I meant to kill you until you showed me that you were a truthful man.

I never met a man before who would not do anything to a woman that she did not want done to her. You must have strong moral convictions and tremendous self-control. So in my mind you have become a hero worthy of respect and admiration. You were kind and compassionate toward me when everything in your carnal nature told you to take me for your own desires. It is those memories of your goodness and the warmth of my daughter that helped me sleep at night and pursue my daily activities.

It has not been easy for us. What kept me going—keeps me in that valley—is not wanting to condemn my daughter to being a slave. There is nothing about her that makes her look any different from white girls. She has beautiful hair. It is golden and I curl it. On the slave market, she would fetch high dollar. My scars are the only mark on her. Her eyes are light and she is smart. Of course I think there is no girl alive, or who has ever lived—who equals her beauty.

If she and I were not in our valley, my scars and her beauty would be our curses. I once thought about going to Missouri, for there I can be granted a pass to leave the state and go to Illinois or Iowa. I don't know what I would do in a free state. Perhaps I could find work as a servant, but I just cannot bring myself to risk it. In our valley, I know I can disappear in these wooded acres with my daughter like a doe with her fawn. I will not have her be the property of any man.

No slave has a legal right to refuse her owner sex. I refused you, and you did not exercise your right to take me even though the law said it was within your power to do so. I realized the night you dreamed I was on top of you that you would have made love to me if only I had asked. I had a fleeting notion that I would be your wife. No slave can expect to become a wife to her master…

I have cried at night with no one to comfort me. I have cried in the morning with no one to encourage me. What would you have done with me in New York?

She has a name, Cry. I should have told you that already. I named her Alyx Eve. Memaw's middle name was Eve. That's not the only reason I named her Eve. I figure her to be the first woman in our family to go to college in America. I have given up on that dream of mine, but I will have it for her.

I do have a reason to be happy. Eve was past three last April when I looked down toward the river and saw a woman, walking slowly toward the cabin. I ran to meet her, crying, shouting, and stopping a couple of times to make sure. When I knew it was my mother, I can't tell you what joy ran through me.

That afternoon, I learned about Lincoln's Emancipation Proclamation. She had been bought by a cotton grower in Mississippi. When she learned that she was free, she did not follow the other slaves who had no homes to become contraband, tagging along after the soldiers who were responsible for their being free. She came home to Kentucky.

How sad it made me to hear her say that slaves in Union slave states were not freed. That meant she had come home to a place where she could become a slave again. Like me, she never will be enslaved again.

Picking cotton has been so hard on her. I cry as I write this. She is so frail. Her hands are rough, cracked open like the earth in a drought. Her eyes do not have the life in them now that I remember. She is a blessing though and she loves Eve.

In November of this year, Eve ran into the house and I knew someone was approaching the cabin. I went to the door and sure enough two women were almost *half way across the clearing. My sisters, Anna and Agatha, had come home from New Orleans. They did not have enough money laid back from their regular Johns, as they called them, when they found out that they were free to leave the brothel, but they saved what they could until they were able to run away. They got on a steamboat and came up the Mississippi to St. Louis then rode another steamer to Louisville.*

How happy my mother was that day. Her three oldest daughter's were at home with her again. I don't have the heart to tell her that we don't own the farm. I have told my sisters and we watch diligently for the rightful owner, Sara, or someone she has sold the property to, to come claim it.

Of my sisters, Allie and Angie, there has been no word. However, my baby sister, Ariana, is alive. Anna says she was not sold. Pap took her with him to Indiana. Perhaps his devil heart could not stand to part with her. She was no older than little Eve is now when he sold us.

I am on my way to Indiana to bring Ariana home. I was across the tracks from you, waiting for a north bound train to take me across the river when I saw you. I have always been one to believe that things happen for a reason. It was meant for me to see you, but not to get up with you.

Perhaps someday there will be a way for people to talk to each other the way a telegraph sends words across a wire, but I mean voices talking and ears hearing the words and recognizing the speaker. How I would like to be able to do that now and hear you... I would like to tell you that I was wrong. In spite of what I told you about only being able to form an attachment with another woman, without one, I get... I should not write these words: but when I need to touch someone—be touched—and there is only me, I never feel like there is another woman making love to me. I always think, dream, know that the man who treated me like a white woman is with me.

Perhaps I should have sent you a telegram.

These are the words I would have sent you: Massa, is ya gwin ta cum git yo proptees and tayk em ta No York whan day war been ofur?

Alyx

Chapter 2

Cry had hoped to be on his way to Kentucky by mid-morning. That did not happen. It was past noon before he was able to get his aunt, his uncle, David and Santos together. He did not get to speak at once as he thought he would.

"I've got to go to Nashville and collect the money for our house," his uncle Wash said. "We don't want to be a burden on you, Cry. Mary and I aim to build us a house..."

"Put your money in gold," Cry interrupted. "Live here like you did when I was gone..."

"Your father needed me. You don't..."

"What did he need you for that I don't?"

His uncle did not speak.

"I see," Cry said, for he understood that his uncle did not wish to mention gun running in front of the others.

"And you don't need me here," his aunt said.

"I need you..."

"For what?"

"My attorney will stop by this afternoon," Cry told her. "He's going to make you my power of attorney..."

His aunt looked at him. He waited for her to say something else. She did not.

"Uncle Wash?"

"Cry?"

"What do you see as the most pressing need in this city?"

"Housing," his uncle answered.

"Then let's start building. I want you to take charge of housing construction. I understand there's been a wartime lapse in construction," Cry said.

His uncle was not at a loss for words.

"Brownstones on Fifth and Madison avenues rent for $320 to $500 per month—twice the prewar level; working-class houses that rented for $40 to $50 per month in 1860 now go for $58 to $83 per month. I know. That's why I said Mary and I would build our own."

"No need," Cry said. "Not soon anyway. I read in the *New-York Times* that would-be tenants have to search like looking for a needle in a haystack to get them for the amounts you quote."

"You serious?"

"I am," Cry said. "This city has poor housing and the demand is high. People don't need to be sold something with tiny air shafts for ventilation."

"They need to get out of boarding houses," his uncle agreed.

"Those who can afford it will buy houses of their own. Let's build houses with private indoor toilets," Cry said.

"Let's do it!"

Cry smiled. He had hoped that his uncle would accept his plan.

"Aunt Mary will control the purse strings," Cry said.

"She's good at that," his uncle laughed.

Mary smiled. She did not have to speak, for her approval was evident to all of them.

"Santos! David!"

"Yes..."

"Yes..."

"This farm is your responsibility. I don't want to lose a foal out of Forrest. Understood?"

"Whatever it takes?" Santos asked.

"Whatever," Cry said.

"I'll do all I can," David said.

"When the attorney leaves this afternoon, Aunt Mary will have five thousand dollars in gold. One thousand of that is mine. One thousand goes to each of you..."

No one spoke. Cry looked from one to the other. Their faces betrayed a wide range of emotions from confusion to disbelief to bewilderment.

"As for mine," Cry said. "I want all of it bet on Goldsmith Mare when she races at Middletown this week. Santos?"

"What, sir?"

Cry flipped an Indian head cent.

"Heads," Santos called.

"Tails," Cry said, kneeling over the coin. "David goes to the first race. You two will alternate. One will stay here with the mares; the other will attend a race."

"Fair enough," Santos said. "I'll send a bet, too, but not all of mine. I'll keep some eggs in my basket."

"I'm not betting," Mary was no longer at a loss for words. "Wash can do as he likes..."

Chapter 3

"May I?" the woman asked.

Cry nodded and moved toward the window. The woman sat beside him.

"You going to Kentucky?"

"Yes," Cry said. "And you?"

"To New Orleans," she said. "I came to Ohio to be with my mother while she died."

"I'm sorry," Cry said as the train began to move.

"It is sad," the woman said. "I am Maria."

"I am Cry..."

"I am from Italy..."

"The south," Cry said.

"How do you know?"

"I grew up with friends from there. They sang and danced. You remind me of Henri's sister..."

"My family has gypsy blood. They never live in one place. I am called Madam Maria in New Orleans. Let me see your hands."

Cry turned his palms up and reached toward the woman.

"Your heart line shows that you are empty," she whispered. "In the old country, I understand that what was sensible and understood about love has also been lost..."

She looked at Cry, pursed her lips, and looked back at his hands, first the left and then his right...

"The gods came down from Mount Olympus. With no feeling, they took women. As mortals, some men, although forbidden to do as the gods, take women. You are not ruled by compulsion nor ensnared by the Fates. You know loneliness..."

"Do you tell the same story to every man you meet?"

"I can read the stars, the sun and the moon, read the cards, or gaze into a ball, but no story is the same."

"Every story ends the same way..."

"In death, I suppose," she answered. "But there is also an eternal story, and to guide us, the old mythologies. Your fate line ties into your life line. It tells me that there are circumstances that are beyond your control. You have many events recorded on your life line. I see that you will live a long time, but there will be many more events. You have lost someone, and you will lose more in two days. The people will not be your family. She lives by her instincts..."

"Who?" Cry asked.

"The woman you journey towards; the one you lost years ago," Maria said. "She has a sense of place, but she has no deep, how do I say it? No hope without you... You do not live by your hands, but with your mind. You are escaping, always escaping. That is why you must create... What? Only you can say... You gave her new eyes for viewing this land of chains. Before she could locate the secret of her womanhood, she was taken from you."

"You are good," Cry said. "Is this where you ask for money?"

Maria laughed. "If I were asking for money, I would have said that for one dollar in gold I would answer two questions. I would have also said that I would only answer: *yes* or *no,* then I would have told you that for five dollars, gold, I would answer four questions or I would have asked you to lay five dollars, gold, in your hand and told you to make three wishes. Your lack of confidence in me will mean that your story remains untold."

"Tell me what I am," Cry said.

She did not hesitate to answer, "You are all men who have scanned the horizon for game, for the enemy, and have fought. As for romance, you want to learn that from a woman, the woman you seek..."

"And who is this woman I seek?"

"The slave," she answered.

Cry sat silent; the woman watched him and traced lines in his hands.

"You have escaped death twice..."

Cry nodded before he could stop himself, remembering the man who shot him and took Alyx, and remembering how Rebel went down after he crossed the field and the men who chased him did not follow. He also remembered the hotel room when all guns were aimed at him and the men on the steamboat talking about John Brown..."

"You will escape death one more time. You will not think that you will escape it, but you will..."

"Enough," Cry said.

Maria gripped his fingers.

"Men who love women and women who love men seldom meet as the two of you did," she whispered. "Their most important journeys are inward. Their outward searches are for those things that give meaning to their lives. Love is an emotion. Integrity is a conviction. I can't tell you why you were born or she was born. I can only tell you that a woman who loves men is subtle like the scent of honeysuckle in late summer. She is honest and self-sacrificing, qualities you find appealing, you can't help but love her. You must never stop loving her, but she will die if you do not hurry..."

"How?" Cry asked.

"I can't say," she said, then got up and walked away.

Chapter 4

When the conductor entered the passenger car from the front, Cry knew he would announce the next stop, his...

"Next stop, Lebanon," the man shouted.

"May I?" Madam Maria asked, having approached from the rear of the car.

"Certainly," Cry said.

"You have an aura of evil surrounding you," she said. "I could not let you get off without sharing the rest of what I have seen..."

"I don't know how you did it," Cry began...

"Let me show you," she said, taking his left hand. "See that," she continued, tracing lines that crossed.

"Yes..."

"And your right hand," she said, tracing a second set of lines. "A Cross Mystique that lies in the center of the quadrangle between Head and Heart lines shows your strong psychic sense. That is how I know what I know. Your right hand is you future. Your left hand is what you were born with. I have the Crescent of Intuition... Here... See this?"

"I see," Cry said.

"I have this extra sense. I can perceive when I hold a psychic hand... Hands like yours..."

"So you know what I think…"

"Some believe that. Sometimes I only feel what the psychic person feels, but you…"

"What?"

"You have many fine spidery lines," she explained, taking both his hands, holding them.

"You did not choose to kill the one nor find the woman," she whispered.

"You can't know that," Cry said, shaking his hands free from hers.

"His chariot is magnificent," she whispered. "I am a spiritualist. I can't help you. Even though I work with God, I can't change what is to be…"

Cry looked into her eyes. They blazed.

"Your left hand tells me those things. Your right hand tells me things you need to know…"

"What things?"

"What you wanted to know from your grandfather. It was a custom, back in his time, if a child in the family died, the child to follow would be given its name so *little so and so* might return. This happened twice in your large family…"

"The yadicone," Cry said.

"Her mother was Gambian by blood, though removed by generations. *Ya* means you come before. *Dicone* means name child this… Yadicone is a spirit child fated to a cycle of early death and rebirth to the same mother. In Wollof, the word captures the two loves, the dead child's dual world. The spirit child is a question mark suspended between the terrestrial and spiritual poles. Today he is on mundane soil, enjoying the fruits of law and order, but tomorrow he will be in the spiritual realm where all is mysterious."

"Why do you tell me this?"

"Because it is written in your right hand," she said.

Cry looked at his palm...

"What makes the yadicone powerful is not the riddle of his comings and goings, but the feeling he leaves with his mother. He was dark, this yadicone. She killed him and the next child, the woman you bought, was born white. Jujus, oracles, the devil nor God can save that mother. The yadicone does not care. His ears are blocked to her endless mournings. He will get there before you do and he will show no mercy."

"You are good," Cry said.

"I am what I am," she said. "If others could read your hands, they would want what I want."

"And what is that?"

"They would want you to get to her; give her hope; and give her a long life with God. She deserves to grow old and raise children. She has suffered so much. She is a hero for all she's gone through. Don't let her end in tragedy!"

Chapter 5

Cry bought two horses, saddles, blankets, and other tack in Lebanon. He did not tarry. He rode hard and spent the night on the river bank at Tebbs Bend between Campbellsville and Columbia.

The following morning, he studied the map Alyx had drawn for him. She had drawn the river without printed directions, but she had indicated north and used arrows to guide him.

It was a warm morning. The sky toward the west was dark as he broke camp, but toward the east, the sunrise painted the clouds red.

He was anxious to tell Alyx that Berea College had reopened. He could not conceal his joy. He whistled as he rode, following a wide path created by ancient herds, the mammoth and the more recent buffalo and deer.

As he rode, the sky grew darker and the day appeared more like twilight than morning. As he rode, the gentle breeze became a wind, steadily intensifying until dead limbs began to fall, some with a resounding crash. The horse he rode, a bay, snorted and pranced. Cry knew the horse feared the gathering storm.

Toward the west, the black clouds glowed orange and lightning flashed, striking downward or running cloud to cloud. Cry got down from the bay and stepped his left foot in the stirrup of the saddle on the older horse, a roan he had chosen for Alyx and her daughter to ride if, indeed, she and the child wanted to return to Lebanon with him, then take the first train to Cincinnati...

The bay attempted to bolt but only succeeded in jerking Cry upward. He held the reins and groped for the other stirrup. When the bay reared, he regained his balance and planted his right foot firmly in the wooden stirrup. He pulled the frightened animal down on all four legs again and wrestled her alongside where she began to follow the roan step for step.

He could no longer study the map. From what he could remember, visualize, he needed to pass three other streams that fed into the Green River from the north and he should find the farm in the valley beyond...

The wind stopped blowing. A hush fell over the forest. Cry spurred the roan into a gallop. The bay, calm now, followed, her rhythm smooth, natural.

In the eerie silence, Cry gave the roan more rein. The animal fell into a full gallop, smooth as a rocking chair. Cry felt the adrenaline rush he had felt each time he rode into battle with Pap. As the roan crossed the first stream, Cry remembered the grey horse with the cropped ear. He remembered Maria's palm reading, the aura of evil she said surrounded him, and the Yadicone. He saw that the valley beyond the stream was narrow. He could see the second creek.

The roan crossed the second stream, leaping sure footed. The valley opened. To his right, green fields and a stone chimney, straight and tall, were the only signs that remained of a once productive farm, a victim of the late war. Cry did not have to spur the roan or give him more rein, for the animal had settled into his best gait and the bay mare offered no resistance.

As they raced toward the third stream, the wind picked up. In front of them, Cry heard the roar moving from the southwest. Lightning flashed. Thunder roared like cannons. A buck came up the bank of the creek as the roan reached it. The bay broke to the right and Cry let her go rather than risk being unseated. The roan, undaunted, raced down, across, and then up the opposite bank.

The fury of the storm raged northeasterly across the valley. Midnight could have been no darker than it became in a few moments. The roan fell forward. Cry knew the horse was dead, but he dared not jump. In the rain that fell in torrents, the roan slid across the field then came to a slow stop.

Cry crawled off the horse toward the right and lay down as close to the large body as he could, thinking: *this is where I will die.* The air was thick, filled with swirling debris, grass blades lethal as darts, mud, and things he could not see: trees, creek gravel from the riverbed, animals, alive, crying out in pain above him. For a moment, some of the screams sounded human...

Chapter 6

Although the roar of the tornado seemed to last for hours, in a few minutes the darkness lifted, but the rain kept falling, lightning flashed in the storm's wake. Cry could hear the roar, moving northeast like a train at top speed.

He stood. The roan looked like a unicorn, the stake that killed him protruding from the center of his skull. There was no sign of the mare. He looked toward the river. The tornado had dipped down into the water or on the river bank for there was no sign of it upstream or in the trees across Green River. Its swath was wider than the valley, but not by much. Trees beyond the clearing and behind him, some broken, some uprooted, lay in all directions, crisscrossed, entangled by the rotation of the wind.

While he lay face down, shielded by the roan, his only hope was that Alyx's map was incorrect, that the valley he was in was not hers. When he looked to his right, he knew it was her valley. A partially destroyed chimney, laid up from river and field stone, marked the spot where the cabin had stood. As he rushed toward the chimney, he saw that only the floor remained, swept clean except for the area in front and to the right of the chimney. Stones lay in a heap upon the wet boards.

Beyond the field, in what had been the edge of the forest, Cry saw the rubble of a pole barn. He ran toward it, crawling over, under, and through the mangled trees.

"Alyx!" he called.

He listened. There was no answer. There was no roof on the barn. On the top timbers, four white hens sat.

They thought it was night he thought. *They went to roost...When the roof left, they kept their backs toward the storm.* He could tell that because the feathers had been plucked from their backs and wings. They did not move as he made his way through the barn. He found a cow in the only stable. He opened the stall door, but the cow would not come out. He propped the door open with a broken timber and made his way toward the field, moving beyond the house, following a trail of household debris.

He had not walked far from the chimney, in the direction the roar had gone, before he found the first body, her legs stripped of flesh from the knees down. A few yards away and to the right, he found the second body, crushed as though a heavy tree had fallen on her, but there was no tree, for it had been picked up again. Beyond the field, in the trees hardest hit, splintered snags for the most part where virgin timber less than fifteen minutes earlier had towered, he found the older woman he knew was Alyx's mother. Her face, frozen in fear, was the only part of her that distinguished her as human.

"Alyx," he called, following the storm's path, a trail of logs from the house, some with newspaper wallpaper still attached.

Where the storm had gone back into the sky, he saw Alyx. Even at a distance, he could see how beautiful she was... She wore a dress, a store bought dress with blue flowers on it and a velvet bonnet with white lace. The dress was wet and muddy, but it was not torn. Alyx sat upright, her face, legs, and arms unscathed...As he knelt by her, there was no doubt in his mind that she was dead.

Chapter 7

"Amen..." the minister said, then walked toward Cry's aunt and spoke softly to her. Whatever he told her seemed to comfort her. He shook hands with Wash, David and Santos. Then he approached Cry.

"Thanks," Cry said, shaking his hand.

"Your cemetery is filling fast..."

"Much too fast," Cry agreed. "Aunt Mary will take you to the house. We expect you to eat..."

"That's not necessary..."

"Follow her," Cry directed. "Let us finish what we have to do and we will join you..."

"I've never seen a cast iron casket before," Reverend Sweeney said. "And her tombstone... I like it. That is a fine epitaph, Cry. Did you come up with it?"

"No," Cry answered. "And the casket was the only one the undertaker in Campbellsville had that was suitable for transporting a body by train. They're waiting for you and I need to help the men. Go on now..."

As Cry walked toward the open grave, Eve tugged at his left hand.

"What is it, child?"

"Will you be my daddy, Cry?"

He looked down into her light eyes as Alyx had described them in her letter...

"Of course, darling," he said, picking her up.

Chapter 8

The next morning, Santos rushed into the house, calling, "We've got a dandy!"

"What is it? Cry asked, pushing his chair back from the table.

"It's a stud!"

"Yes!" Cry exclaimed.

Eve got up to follow Cry and Santos. At the paddock, she climbed the wooden fence and sat on the square post. Cry lifted her down and put her on his shoulders. In a few minutes, Wash and Mary joined them. David led the mare from the barn. Her foal, black with four stockings and a blazed face, wobbled next to her side.

"He's a keeper," David called. "Look at those legs..."

"He'll be seventeen hands," Cry said.

"Every bit of it," Santos agreed. "Got a name for him yet, Cry?"

"Champ," Cry said.

"The Mare runs at Ploughkeepsie this weekend," Wash said.

"Put a thousand of mine on her," Cry said and turned toward his aunt.

"How about you, Wash?" she asked.

"Five hundred," he answered.

"Santos has my money," David said. "How about you, Mary?"

"I'm risking my thousand like Cry," Mary smiled.

Chapter 9

In the afternoon, Cry returned from the city and went up to his room. He did not have time to put away the things he had bought before he heard David calling, "Cry, you've got to come down here!"

"What's happened?" Cry asked, fearing the worst. "Is it the mare or the colt?"

"Neither," David said as Cry rushed downstairs. "You ain't gonna believe it!"

"Try me!"

"You've got to come to the barn," David said and rushed from the house, Cry passing him as they crossed the porch.

"Where's everybody?"

"In the barn!"

Cry broke into a run. He vaulted the gate when he reached it. David opened it and walked through. Cry stopped...

"You were right," Cry said. "It's too good to be true..."

"They got here right after you left," David said, pointing.

"Cry!" his mother shouted.

Cry rushed toward her. They hugged. He could feel her tremble. Forrest nickered.

"I don't have one, old fellow," Cry said.

"Here," Santos said, reaching toward him with a quartered apple in his hand.

Cry went to the stable and opened the door. Forrest rushed past him and ran down the hallway of the barn, kicking his heels like a colt then turning and running back toward them at top speed. He stopped, his nose inches from Cry's outstretched hand, and ate the fruit.

"How did we get so lucky?" Cry asked without turning to face his mother.

"I told them to wait for you, son. Just so you all know, I had to come home. The British made a raid, rounded up all the Fenians they could find. They took Patrick, but they missed me. That's all I'm ever going to say about it..."

"I'm sorry, mother," Cry said.

"Don't be," she answered. "Let's step out of the way. Forrest needs to run. We've got the mares up. Champ is beautiful..."

"The next one is yours..."

"No!"

Cry stepped back to let Forrest go out, then looked at his mother.

"The next one is Eve's. It's on its way now," she said. "Let's get out of here so Santos and David can tend to business."

Chapter 10

In the light of a full moon, Cry walked to the cemetery. A light breeze blew against his back. He opened the iron gate—left it open—and walked to his father's grave; stood there in silence; went to Jeff's grave and bowed his head; and walked to the tombstone at his father's feet. As he had promised the woman, there was no name, no dates, only the words: *A Friend* that he read as a cloud began to cover the moon.

"It was nice of you," his mother's voice startled him, " to let David bury his mother here."

"He told you?" Cry asked, no longer worried about how he would explain Jane's presence.

"He did," she answered, placing her left arm around his waist. "I've decided..."

"What?" Cry asked after she did not continue.

"We Irish are a strange bunch, aren't we?"

"You don't feel strange to me," he said, pulling her closer with his right arm that he had dropped down and around her shoulder.

"The Irish led the riots here when Lincoln called for the draft. Maybe it is true that we never meant to be citizens— only came here to stay until the British are driven out of Ireland, then we'll go back. When I say: *we,* I don't mean I'll go back. When I say: *we,* I don't mean I'd listen to the Pope before I'd listen to or follow an American President..."

"You don't have to explain anything to me."

"I sold my land. Forrest will have at least two foals on Irish soil, son. The filly's as fine as your stud colt, Champ. Eve calls her Ari. The colts from Forrest will be all the history we can make in Ireland. I've talked to Wash. He told me about building..."

"Slow down," Cry said. "Whatever you want, I'll help you do it or get it..."

"I'm sorry about what happened in Kentucky... I'm proud of you for the way you've taken to Eve. We've talked. She's taken to you. You know they're really Irish, too. That's what we'll tell everybody. That Eve's a doll."

"I'm glad you're home," Cry said. "I really like the fact that I don't have to come to Ireland for Christmas."

"I'm tired," she said. "I think I'll turn in."

"I'll be along shortly," Cry said. "I'm going to be here a while and at the barn. I want to put Forrest up."

"I'll see you in the morning..."

Cry watched her walk away. The sky was clear. He watched her cross the lawn and go up the steps of the front porch, then he walked to the grave on Jeff's left and looked down. He could read the words:

A. Day

1847-1866
No More Tears. No Scars.

As the flame from the lantern he, David and Santos installed flickered, he thought *I wasn't much of a knight. I wish it didn't have to be this way. My mind is racing. I've got to remember to thank David for what he said* Cry's mind jumped from one thought to another until he realized that the woman was David's mother. *That's why she was at the barn with him...*

The silence of the cemetery seemed fitting as he returned to his father's grave. The wind had laid. Cry looked up in order to stop feeling, for pain, the nagging kind that devours joy, was all he felt when he looked back down at his father's grave. Looking up, the remorse was less agonizing than the pain of knowing, of death, that looking down brought to him. The stars directly overhead were invisible, erased by the moon light.

"There is nothing more that I can think of to say that I did not say to you when I came home," he finally said. "I could not believe when I placed my ear against your chest that your heart was not beating. There is such a sting to this I would not have imagined..."

He heard Forrest nickering.

"I'm coming, Old Man," he called without looking toward the barn, without looking down, turning...

"I brought him an apple," Alyx said. "Your mother asked me to bring it."

"Thanks," Cry said, rushing toward the gate where she stood. "Are you sure you should be up?"

"Tell me how it was," she said.

"I came up to the house after I had found your sisters and your mother, remembering your voice when we were on the steamboat going upriver, saying: *There was a trap door that led down into the cellar...* I knew your hiding place would have been to the left or the right of the fireplace, depending on where the steps were. When I moved the chimney rocks from the floor and found the trap door on the right and lifted it, my heart raced. I called your name. I heard a child crying. I told myself it was Eve..."

"I remember," Alyx said, "hearing you call: Come out. It's over."

"You came up with Eve in your arms. I said: Here...Let me help you and I tried to lift her from you..."

"She would not come to you."

"No."

"I remember standing up beside you..."

"They didn't get down, you kept screaming."

"I'll never forget that," she sobbed.

"In time, maybe," he said. "Eve would not stop crying. I looked at the two of you. I had seen men after battle with the same look on their faces, in their eyes..."

" It seems like I kept saying: we've got to find them!"

"You did. I kept telling you to take care of her, for I had found them already."

"I'm sorry," she said.

"Don't be. While you and Eve looked for the mare, I carried the bodies to the house site and down into the cellar. I could not take Ariana down. She looked just like you did when we were on the boat, except she had no scars and her eyes were blue...When I saw those eyes, I knew where to look... Afterwards, I went to the river and waded it until I was in up to my shoulders so I could get as much blood out of my clothes before it dried as I possibly could. Carrying the three of them reminded me of the men I helped bury at Missionary Ridge and after the Battle of Nashville."

"Tell me how you buried them. I've had that on my mind since I've been here. Whatever your doctor gave me, it knocked me out."

"I thought it best to have him give you something strong. Are you sure you want to hear the rest?"

"Tell me," she said.

"Twice, I started to climb down the steps with Ariana on my shoulder, but I could not make myself descend... Having found no hoe, no shovel to dig graves, I figured the cellar was a ready made tomb, but I wanted to bury Ariana here for your sake, near Jeff and my father. I used the stones that had fallen into a pile, sealing you and Eve inside, to seal the entrance to the cellar. I restacked the stones in a solid column, the larger stones placed on the two top steps of sandstone, level bases that will support the weight of that pillar. I laid the stones one upon the other until they reached to a point within four inches of the top. Then I crossed the floor to the point where the entrance would have been and tugged at a large, carved river slate stone which had served as a step outside the cabin door and I used it to seal the grave. I closed the trap door. If you want to go back and rip up the floor, we will and take David and Santos with us. We can tear down the chimney and build a wall around the cellar top..."

"Could we have brought them, too?"

"No," he said, without going into detail. "When I turned to look toward the spot where the roan lay, I saw you and Eve, with the mare. I had not expected you to be so lucky as to find the horse much less catch her."

"You ran toward us..."

"I didn't want you to go back up there."

"You told me we'd be going back the way you came as soon as you got the saddle off the roan."

"You wanted to know if I aimed to carry it out?"

"You said you were going to put it on the cow…I remember most of what happened after that. I should have thanked you for bringing her here…"

"You did," he said. "David and Santos will take care of her. If she never wants to come out of her stable, she never has to…"

"It was as though Ariana knew someone was coming that day. She said her nose was itching like it never had before… She got up early, put on her new dress, and sang or whistled until the tornado came down on us. She made us go into the cellar first."

"When I found Ariana and thought I had found you, I blamed myself. I blamed my father."

"You are neither to blame. It is useless for me to say this, but I think it— feel like it should have been me," she told him as he closed the gate after she walked through. "But I've said that… Ariana hated me for coming to get her. My aunt was pleased. She had told her she had to leave anyway after Pap's funeral. Me, I felt like I was meant to go get her that very day. She had nowhere to go. She couldn't have made it on her own unless she used her body. I know that. She knew that, too, and stopped hating me after we got home. Although she had no way of knowing what it is like to be a slave, she took to Eve and soon became less fragile with the rest of us. She began to remember how it was before Pa drowned. Her happiness was short lived..."

"I haven't meant to ignore you."

"I know you haven't," she said. "You have been denying yourself..."

"Why do you say that?"

"I have not seen you do one thing for yourself, but all I hear from everyone here is how much you have done for them."

"I have yet to do something for you."

"You have done everything already," she said.

"Come here, fellow," Cry called as he opened the gate to the paddock.

"I'll get the barn door," Alyx said, "and his stable door, too, while you feed him. Just tell me which one is his..."

"Second on the left," Cry answered.

Forrest ate the apple hurriedly and ran into the barn, into his stable, and Alyx closed the door behind him.

Cry waited at the gate for her. After she had closed the barn door, she joined him.

"Before you tell me," Cry said, as he closed the gate, "the answer is: no, you are not..."

"I am not what?"

"Moving out," Cry said. "Eve told me you aim to..."

Alyx stopped. She did not say anything.

"And for your information, lady," he said, "I bought myself some things today…"

"Clothes?" she asked.

"No," he said. "I figure to take you and Eve shopping for clothes tomorrow. I might even buy a suit as well. I bought an easel, paint, brushes, and canvases today."

"Do you think you might need a model?" she asked, thrusting her hand into his side.

He looked down at her hand and saw the dagger…

"Do you know where I might find one?" he asked.

She pricked his side.

"I just might happen to know the right woman," she laughed. "And her hips are still small."